The
Juggernaut
Tales from the Juggernaut

Peter A Dixon

Author's Note: This is a work of fiction. Names, characters, places, and incidents are a product of the author's imagination. Locales and public names are sometimes used for atmospheric purposes. Any resemblance to actual people, living or dead, or to businesses, companies, events, institutions, or locales is completely coincidental.

The Juggernaut / Peter A Dixon -- 1st ed.
ISBN 9781521422410

For MJ

Now or Never

Contents

Prologue

Tila ran through the gleaming corridors of the brand new colony ship *Rising Star* with the intense focus and careless abandon that only an eight-year old girl can muster.

The one-eyed head of her stuffed bear, along for the ride, rocked back and forth with every footstep. Its threadbare mouth fixed in a perpetually bemused expression.

Tila danced between adult legs which were a forest of sharply pressed uniforms, crisp and spotless. A sparse canopy of clipboards and portable computers shielded her from the twin tracks of lighting recessed into the ceiling as she ran on toward the bridge.

On the bridge, Captain Grace Vasquez turned to one of the two view screens which provided *Rising Star* with direct communication to her two sister ships *Far Horizon* and *New Dawn*. The captain stood tall and straight, smartly dressed in her crisp white uniform. Her long dark hair was tied back in a tight braid with not a single strand out of place.

On the view screen showing her the bridge of the *Far Horizon* the captain watched a man bent low over a console, concentrating on something inscrutable. He rested his chin in his hands and his elbows on the desk as he read the results of the tenth simulation he had performed that morning. His brow furrowed as he read the numbers again.

The captain tapped a control to switch the scene from a wide shot of the other bridge to the personal camera on the man's console.

She knew he was running calculations again.

"How are we looking, Professor?" she asked.

He didn't look up from his screen but took advantage of the distraction to flex the stress from his shoulders before answering. "I think it's going to work."

The captain spoke in a tone of mock horror. "You think? Is that the best you can do? After years of planning and the trillions this mission cost? You think?"

The man looked directly into the camera. "You're welcome to come over here and check my figures."

"Love to. Can't. Too busy." She made a show of checking her own console before a smile broke across her face.

He smiled back, "So we'll stick with my best guess, shall we? It *is* going to work, you know."

"I know. You wouldn't give the mission commander the green light unless you were sure."

"Or my wife," he winked.

"I should hope not, Thomas!" She bent over the console and wiggled the fingers of her left hand at the camera. Light flashed from the slim gold band around her finger. She blew him a kiss.

He recoiled in pretend shock. "Grace! Not in front of the crew!"

Grace grinned and stood tall once more and clasped her hands behind her back. "Attention all bridge crew! Anybody wishing to make a formal complaint about their captain's conduct on the bridge with her civilian husband while we are still in Commonwealth space should address their concerns to the XO. I will give your concerns my utmost attention when our mission here is complete. Is that understood?"

Her executive officer, a lean wiry man with cropped grey hair and a face so stern people assumed upon first meeting him that he had never heard of a sense of humour said, "Captain, by the time our mission is complete we will no longer be under the jurisdiction of any Commonwealth systems."

"Emest, protocol must still be followed."
He kept his face perfectly straight, masking the smile that danced behind his eyes. Grace had worked with her XO long enough to appreciate his wonderful sense of humour first hand, and respect that he could switch to deadly serious when the situation demanded.

It was just one of the reasons he made such a fine first officer.

"Yes ma'am. I also believe that all bridge officers and crew are performing their duties to the best of their abilities and will be unlikely to report any..uh..fraternizing at this time, ma'am."

"Understood. Carry on."

Her husband pointed at something above her head. "Maybe your bridge crew won't cause us any trouble but I think I see someone who might."

"Do you think it's the troublemaker we caught spying on us over breakfast this morning?" she whispered conspiratorially without turning around.

"I do. And I'm beginning to have concerns about the security on your flagship when anyone can just waltz onto the bridge when they feel like it."

Grace turned around to see a dark haired little girl watching from the viewing gallery.

The girl was searching the room for someone but struggling to locate them in the expanse of the busy command deck. Behind her stood a Master-at-Arms who shrugged at the captain and then snapped out a salute.

The girl's small face pressed against the glass partition. Her quick, excited breaths fogged the cold surface. At last she found who she was looking for and waved at the captain. Then she raised a stuffed animal above her head and wiggled its paw in greeting also.

"Security!" said the captain, "Please stop indulging my daughter."

Tila rode an elevator down to the main bridge level to join her mother. Grace met her at the door with her hands on her hips and barred her way. "Now you know you shouldn't be up here young lady," she said. A smile took the edge of her stern tone. This was her daughter, after all, and this was a very big day. "Your father is very busy right now. His work is nearly finished."

"I wanted to see," Tila pleaded. She looked like a miniature copy of her mother apart from her hair. Where Grace's hair was neatness and military discipline Tila's hair has billowed behind her during her run and was now plastered all over her face. The effect was also spoilt somewhat by the bear hanging from her hand. "Hi daddy!" She waved vigorously at her father's image.

Her father waved back. "Hello princess. You're going to be good like we discussed and stay out of trouble, aren't you?"

Tila nodded absently and wobbled on the points of her toes as she tried to get a better view of the control room. She pawed stray locks of hair from her eyes.

"It's boring back there," she said.

Her mother stepped away from her work, knelt down beside Tila. She smoothed her palms across her daughter's face to part the remaining hairs and finger combed them back into place.

"Soon it won't be boring," she said, "But for now you have to watch from the gallery with the other children. And you will have a much better view of the stars from the observation dome."

On the *Far Horizon* a technician apologetically 'ahemed' his way to her husband's side. "I'm sorry, sir, but it's time."

Her father nodded. "Time to go now, princess."

The aide exchanged words with the captain of the *Far Horizon* then spoke into a communicator clipped to his uniform, "All stations commence final preparations."

Orange hazard lights sprang to life on all three bridges simultaneously and an artificial voice announced, "Time is minus ten minutes to Jump. Repeat. T minus 10 minutes."

"I'll see you both on the other side," Thomas said to his family.

Tila pouted, but despite the tiny frown that wrinkled her forehead her sulkiness was not heartfelt.

Her mother kissed it away. "Come on now, off you go." Tila held up her stuffed animal for a kiss too. Grace smiled and kissed the toy to indulge her daughter one last time.

"Be good," she said to Tila, "It's going to get very busy in here. You have to go now, honey." Tila nodded. They had told her this was a very important day, and she had already promised to be on her best behaviour. Just like her mother she kept her promises.

"Look," added her mother, "this will be over soon. When it is I'll come and find you and we can find your star together. Deal?"

Her daughter gave this weighty matter serious consideration over another frown.

"Promise," she said. It wasn't a question.

Her mother smiled at the way her little girl could take charge of a situation when she wanted something and wondered if she was any different at that age. She held her daughter's chin between her finger and thumb and looked her directly in the eye. "Tila, when this is all over I promise I'll find you."

Grace held Tila's hand as they walked back to the elevator together. She kissed Tila on the forehead one last time, stood up and pressed the button to close the glass doors.

Sudden quiet enveloped Tila as the door seals muffled the increasing volume coming from the bridge of the colony ship.

"Promise?" she mouthed again at her mother through the glass.

The elevator rose swiftly and smoothly, separating them.

"I promise," her mother mouthed back across the growing distance. She blew her daughter a final kiss as she vanished from sight.

Meanwhile, the bridge had sprung into action like a beehive under attack.

Huge screens overhead displayed mission critical data beneath schematic outlines of the three colony ships. Below each schematic another screen displayed a large translucent cone on the black background. The vertex sat in the lower left of the display and the base in the upper right.

The colours graduated from green at the point to red at the base. A sharp, white line sprang from the vertex to the centre of the base and wavered almost imperceptibly, like a nervous conductor before a big concert. Next to the cone numbers flashed by too fast to read.

Below this double layer of screens a wider display spanned the bridge. On this the images of the three cones were stacked on top of one another. Each one trembled in time with its counterpart, and as the seconds passed the trembling faded, the images aligned, and the conductor steadied.

More number sequences bordered the cones on the wide display but all were close to zero, and falling fast. As the numbers crept closer to zero the images of the three cones sharpened until they were almost a perfect match.

On the bridge of the *Far Horizon* a technician addressed Tila's father. "Sir, the quantum cores are in ascendance. We have cross checked the stochastic simulations and we are holding at a ninety-seven percent probability of success."

"Margin?"

"Less than point one two percent."

Thomas spoke to his wife. "It's not going to get any better than this, is it? What's that phrase you like so much? Now or never?"

Grace nodded. She put aside the role of wife and mother and spoke as captain to the first officer. "Begin final sequence for Jump to Baru."

The XO repeated the order into his console microphone. "We have a go for Jump. Repeat, we are go."

A klaxon sounded across the bridge and the overhead screens changed to prioritise the schematic displays of the three colony ships.

Around the bridge crew members called out checks and counter-checks in sequence. Each person finally performing for real what had been simulated a hundred times. The stations sounded off one by one, each call bringing the ships a moment closer to their destiny.

"Has fleet network been established?"

"Network is locked and coded, sir."

"Engines?"

"Ready."

"Jump Drive is online and operating within normal parameters."

"Gravimetric compensation is available."

"Stochastic models have been confirmed and verified."

"Stellar drift check?" said the XO.

"Confirmed. Stellar drift calculations have been finalised and real time simulations are now available."

"*Rising Star* mass displacement has been confirmed," reported a technician.

"Have our sister ships confirmed final mass displacement?" said the captain.

"*New Dawn* mass is in. *Far Horizon* mass coming through. We are synchronizing data among the fleet now," the first officer answered.

"Pilot-wave generator standing by."

"Bohrs-field construct is standing by."

The XO turned and made his final announcement to the captain.

"Ma'am, all systems report nominal. We are ready for system Jump."

Tila's mother nodded once more. This was it. She looked to her husband on the bridge of the *Far Horizon*. Even now, in the seconds before they left, he was checking and rechecking calculations. Six years of planning and he was still nervous. She pressed the button to open comms to his ship, then crossed her hands behind her back.

"Are we ready?"

He swallowed, nodded and crossed his fingers.

"It's all down to luck now," he said, "We're as ready as we can be."

Tila's mother squeezed her hands together and wished it was her husband's hand she held.

"You don't need luck," she told him, then to her own bridge she gave the final order, "Begin final sequence."

"Now or never?" said Thomas.

"Now or never," she replied, and smiled at her husband. "I'll see you in fourteen light years."

The three colony ships appeared to hang motionless against the backdrop of a faint nebula. Delicate blue-white tendrils of cloud stretched across the heavenly scene.

Far below the plane of the three spacecraft, a single planet, wreathed in cloud, orbited the warm yellow sun of Selah. In the foreground dozens of ships swarmed away from the rear of the giant vessels.

Three huge engines made up the aft section of each colony ship. They formed an inverted triangle around the drive core. The engines burst into life and strained against the enormous mass of each ship.

Imperceptible at first, the thrust of the engines slowly overcame the dead weight of the spacecraft and against the infinite ocean of stars the ships began to move. First the *Far Horizon*, and then the *New Dawn*.

Inside the *Rising Star* doors parted to admit Tila and her stuffed companion still running as fast as she could. A dome of reinforced glass and steel dominated the large circular room she entered. Through it she could see *Far Horizon* and *New Dawn* starting their voyage. The last time she had been here their sister ships had been at rest. Now she could observe the parallax motion of the ships against the starry background as their engines roared in silent effort.

The observation dome housed almost two hundred people; an assortment of children, carers, administration staff, and others lucky enough to be idle during the Jump, but whose skills would be essential once they reached their destination. Then the real work of establishing the colony would begin. So too would the plan to make the journey back to Commonwealth space.

Not one was alone. They sat in groups, many lying on their backs, all of them staring upward at the edge of known space, ready to drink in the view of the first new constellations seen in nearly a hundred years.

The *Rising Star* ignited her engines at last, and a low rumble shuddered through the walls and floors of the spaceship. Cheers and whoops filled the room as the ship lurched forward.

A few people, caught off-guard by the sudden movement, almost stumbled, but feet and hands moved on reflex as people steadied themselves and no one fell.

The ship intercom was relaying the final countdown from the bridge.

"8....7....6...."

Someone gamely tried to join in with the countdown but after the first number he faltered into silence against the weight of expectation in the room.

Tila raced for a large unoccupied cushion and dived onto it head first. She kicked and twisted in a graceless effort to flop over onto her back and gazed at the scene above. With a mixture of excitement and fear she wrapped both arms around her stuffed toy, squeezed it tight, and held her breath.

"...5...4...3..."

The room tensed. Tila's spine tingled, and her chest felt like silver. Heightened emotions spread wordlessly from group to group.

Someone near her shivered, not from cold but simply to release the tension of the coming event. She noticed some of the adults were holding their breath, too.

No one spoke again. Even the restless children became still as they sensed the moment was upon them.

"..2..1. Jump engines engaged."

The three huge ships had spread out from each other and they now formed the points of a giant 'V' with the *Rising Star* at the base.

Above Tila's ship and to the right *Far Horizon* had already begun to pull away from its companions. It would be the first to Jump.

Twenty thousand meters ahead of each craft the stars began to shimmer. The distortion points expanded and formed three disks, one in front of each ship, each big enough to swallow the fleet.

The disks bloomed into view from nothing. They unfurled like a flower in the morning sun. The centre of each disk burst like a bubble in slow motion, and the ragged edges peeled

back on themselves, twisting through unknown dimensions until the disk became a
ring, and a new starscape appeared through the
strange portals.

The rim of each halo tinged blue where it
faced the colony ships. The far side tinged red.

The central drive core on each ship ignited
at last, kicking the colony ships forward on a
vector to intercept the centre of their respec-
tive disks.

Far Horizon reached her portal first.

There was no flash. No bright light. No
spectacle. The ship simply glided through the
ring cleanly and calmly, like a knife into water,
and vanished.

The portal collapsed into itself. Translucent
silver-blue petals spiralled back into the noth-
ingness of an infinite point and blinked out of
existence with a flash of impossible colour.

Cheers and shouts erupted around the
bridge of the *Rising Star* as pent-up emotion
breached their dam of professionalism.

Excited crew leaped from their seats
throughout the bridge. The first ship was away.
Now to their left the *New Dawn* begin its own
portal approach.

The *New Dawn's* portal burst open in the
space before it, but this time something was
different. Where the portal for the *Rising Star*

had been strong and steady this one twisted and writhed as if two different solar systems fought to occupy the same space. Fierce lightning raced around the rim of the halo and streamers a thousand miles long flashed out into space.

On the *Rising Star* a priority alert flashed across the screen of the first officer.

"Captain!" he called out, "I'm getting reports of an unstable reading from their portal."

Dozens of alarms and sirens sprang to life across the bridge. Crew who moments before were dancing with excitement dived back into seats, checking status updates, running sensor sweeps and trying to find something, anything, to explain what was happening.

The captain leaned over her command console, knuckles white where they gripped the rail. "What's happening? Report!"

"Ma'am! *New Dawn* is experiencing a pilot wave collapse."

"Will the Bohr's-field hold?"

The answer came in a blinding flash. The *New Dawn* was only partway through portal when the integrity of the event horizon failed.

The halo collapsed in on itself in fits and starts and the ring of lightning turned inward. It stabbed at the colony ship from every point of the circumference in a dizzying pulse of light.

The portal shrank to a point of nothing and exploded. The shock wave blasted out in a sphere of devastation, spitting out the remains of the *New Dawn*.

The portal collapse tore the spacecraft in two and wrenched the superstructure in and through itself into an impossible, sickening knot.

Proximity alarms blared on the *Rising Star's* bridge, each new alert more urgent and more desperate than the one before. The Jump Point failure had thrown the *New Dawn* into the path of the *Rising Star*.

The devastation sent a rapid series of explosions rippling beneath the metal skin of the ships energy systems overloaded, and power conduits, ripped in half by the collapsed portal, sparked life into combusted violently with the explosive gasses and liquids stored within.

A second explosion blasted a gaping hole from one side of the ship to the other, engulfing it in flames which died as quickly as they sprang to life, their fuel dissipating rapidly in the vacuum.

The shock wave slammed into the hull of the *Rising Star* and forced it off course with a sickening lurch. Seconds later the fragmented remains of the *New Dawn* pulverised the *Rising Star*. Sections of hull crumpled under the impact. Sensor arrays ripped from their hard points and spun away into space or vanished beneath the destructive hail.

In the observation dome the screams had already begun.

Children and adults alike cried out in hopeless terror. Their former elation turned to horror as they saw the burning remains of their sister ship heading toward them.

On the bridge the captain shouted orders. "Abort! Evasive manoeuvres!"

Technicians and mission specialists hammered at their controls in desperation, as if mere effort could defy the inevitable. One of them looked at the captain and shook his head.

And with a sad finality the captain realised they would not make it. "Impact!" she shouted, "Brace!"

Alarms sounded throughout the ship. Bulkheads designed to protect against collision or explosive decompression slammed shut all around the bridge, metal jaws snapping closed in rapid succession to protect the precious cargo within. The last seal closed with a crash and wrapped up the command centre in a barricade of steel.

The Jump engines, no longer able to maintain their bridge between the stars, flared one last time, bright and hot. The portal flickered and died.

New Dawn, now stricken and helpless, tumbled toward the *Rising Star*. It traced a slow cartwheel through space, leaving a spiral of smoke and debris in its wake. Fires flared and died in the lifeless vacuum as pockets of oxygen aboard the ship ignited in a brief and sudden fury and died as quickly as they were born.

A trail of lights sparked along the superstructure of the *New Dawn*. They glowed and burst one by one. They raced toward the engines and the primary power core finally exploded, casting a million glittering stars into the velvet night. Then they too were consumed by a fiery white bloom which for one deadly instant formed a new star in the heavens as bright as a nova.

Shrieks and screams surrounded Tila as the observation dome's protective shell slowly closed. The blinding flash of the explosion outside dazzled the room. The white light of a thousand suns blasted away all colour and shadow and hope.

People, young and old, were flung around the room as one ship impaled the other. The stars above, so far away, so peaceful, lurched violently. The impact threw Tila and her cushions across the room. They fell around her, on top of her, burying her. She squealed in fright. It was hot and hard to breathe and the yielding mass of fabric made it impossible to find her feet.

She struggled in panic, found her footing at last, and shoved heavy cushions aside to look up one final time.

The sky was on fire.

The burning, broken command module of the *Rising Star*, no longer attached to the rest of the ship, drifted across the scene. She saw the holes that had been rent through the side of the bridge as she watched the debris, equipment and bodies spill out into space.

A final explosion shook the room and the lights failed.

Now the only illumination was the serene silver glow of a cloudless night sky. Around her the room descended into a nightmare of movement and shadow, screams and cries and prayers, while overhead the dome finally closed, extinguishing the light of the stars and the flames.

1

Twelve years later, Captain Hughes, of the trading ship *Orion*, retained his professional composure despite his full understanding of the report in his lap.

Hughes prided himself on his ability to present to his command crew, and the world at large, a quiet and dignified reserve. He imagined himself to be an adventurer, or an explorer, travelling from world to world, star to star, while single-handedly maintaining the civilisation of the Commonwealth states.

It was a mask maintained no matter what troubles arrived on his bridge. Early in his career he had faced down raiders and terrorists. He had negotiated safe harbour for refugee ships during border conflicts between Peleg and Itzo, two systems still squabbling over past glories. They were no longer the supremely important systems they believed themselves to be. No longer the way back to earth. The route to earth was lost, and their glory days had faded. Now they were nothing more than un-important border systems on the far edge of the Commonwealth.

But the situation before him now was enough to crack the mask.

"How long until main engine failure, Na-talie?" said Hughes.

"Impossible to be certain, sir," said Natalie Simms, his chief engineer. "Power readings are highly unstable and the rate of deterioration impossible to predict."

"Dangerous?"

"That's the good news. The failure is non-cata-strophic. The engines will stop working. We'll lose guidance and propulsion soon but the main power core is unaffected."

"And you are certain it is not something we can repair?"

"I'm sorry, sir, but no. The upgrade was pushed upon us by the higher-ups. They insisted the tech was so reliable there would be no need for extensive training. It wasn't cost effective to maintain. They just swap out the units in dock."

"More cost effective, my ass," said Hughes. He pointed at the local star chart on the main screen. "Do you see any docks in this system, Natalie?"

"No sir, I do not," she said.

The captain clenched and relaxed his jaw, giving his chief engineer a marvellous view of the changing topography of his temple.

Hughes looked around his bridge. It was a small and unimpressive command, but at the end of a long career it was just the kind of thing he wanted. Easy trade routes. No drama. No fuss. So why did his ship have to break down here, of all places?

"Are there any other ships in range able to assist?" he asked the bridge. He already suspected that with his luck so far today the answer would be no.

"Negative, sir," replied Nicholas Rhine, his first officer, "The rest of the fleet has insisted they can't wait for us or they risk losing money on their own cargo."

"Can't or won't? Never mind, it's a rhetorical question."

"No other ships within range have the technical knowledge we need," added Simms.

"I would very much like to be wrong in my assessment, but I believe that leaves us only one option if we are to have any hope of getting out of this system quickly," said Hughes. Help would come, once word finally reached head office, or if he was willing to pay exorbitant fees for someone to recover his ship, but those fees reflected on him as a captain, and he was not about to throw away his long-earned reputation now. Besides, there was his bonus to consider.

"Our options are...limited, sir," said Rhine sourly. He keyed commands into the armrest panel of his chair. The image on the main display changed. The graceful, curving vectors of their intended route through the Celato system to the Kinebar Beacon were replaced by an ugly mass of metal. From this far out it looked like a misshapen potato, a lonely dark grey rock at the bottom of a pond.

And probably covered in scum, too, thought Hughes.

The Juggernaut orbited Celato alone. With no frame of reference and no atmospheric haze to give context to the surface details of the city it was impossible to discern the size and scale of the city itself, or any of the component spacecraft from which it was formed.

The shapes had been mashed together to form the Juggernaut could be shuttles or freighters, pleasure craft or deep space miners. From here Hughes couldn't tell the difference.

The captain touched a control and the image magnified. Now he could see smaller details that betrayed the scale of the monstrosity before him. He could even make out some of the surface features, like cooling towers, engines, and docking bays.

In his years travelling the stars Hughes had seen many examples of beautiful craftsmanship and sleek designs. The Juggernaut was none of those things.

"It's just a mess, isn't it?" the captain said to his first officer. As unattractive as it was he couldn't help but stare. Somehow, despite all appearances to the contrary and their most earnest wishes it was their best hope. "It's like child just crushed every toy ship he could find into one big lump."

"It certainly is, sir," said Rhine.
"What is the population of that thing now, anyway? A hundred thousand?"

"More than that now, Captain," said Simms. "The last I heard it was over three hundred thousand people, although that was some time ago."

"Three hundred...? That many, are you sure, Natalie? When did that happen?"

"I don't know sir, and I'm not sure. No one keeps records. It's just an estimate."

The three senior officers gazed at the display. The image shifted in response to the last offering of their manoeuvring thrusters which slowed the *Orion* in anticipation of her new heading.

Between them they could identify dozens of different ship types; civilian, commercial, industrial and even decommissioned military craft. The chief even spotted parts of a space-station jutting out of the city.

"What a wreck!" exclaimed a crew-member, "Who would want to live there? It looks like a spaceship graveyard!"

"Nobody wants to live there, Ensign," replied Rhine, "That's why the inhabitants are called the dispossessed. They have nowhere else to go."

Fantastic, thought the Captain morosely. I'm stuck with the serious failure of untested equipment, in a system no one wants to travel to but everyone has to travel through. And somewhere in a city in space which looks like the carcass of a giant metal whale, a place where starships go to die, I have to find someone with the knowledge to fix my ship.

But a captain had responsibilities, even here. Hughes cleared his throat and resigned himself to his only option. "Very well, let's get this over with. Set course for the Juggernaut."

2

Deep inside the Juggernaut a young woman raced along a dark corridor. The few light panels which still worked cast their weak glow along the tunnel before her. Darkness crouched in the recesses untouched by the light, and ahead of her the shadows pooled together like black mercury.

It was warm here in the depths of the city, warm and dank. The woman was dressed lightly in loose clothing and she carried only a small bag, strapped close to her body to prevent it leaping about as she ran.

Tucked securely into the straps on her back was what looked like a short pipe, about fifteen inches long. Her dark hair, secured in a tight braid, whipped around her as she pounded the deep and dangerous corridors of the Juggernaut.

Tila was twenty now but she had stopped counting the years since the colony disaster twelve years ago.

She had survived that day, and every day since. Now she was older, leaner, harder.

The little girl was gone.

She was desperately quick. She dodged pipes and ducked low ceilings without slowing her pace or breaking her stride. She stopped at a junction and breathed easy despite the run. A sheen of sweat on her dark olive skin sparkled as it reflected what little light there was in the tunnels.

This was not the first time she had run.

She made her decision and turned left into a new corridor. Yet another monotonous passageway lined with endless doors. She kept running. Under her breath, she began to count.

Seconds later two men burst into the same junction, following the same path, hunting the same quarry. They looked right, then left and saw Tila. They renewed their chase, calling threats and warnings, but they panted with the effort of the pursuit. They overcame the same obstacles as Tila but with far less grace. One ducked too low under a crossbeam and lost his balance. He stumbled into his companion, bringing them both to the ground.

Glancing over her shoulder, Tila watched them clamber to their feet before she rounded another corner and her lips twitched into a rare smile.

She found an open doorway and hopped through, and then she stopped.

Wrong door.

Dead end.

She poked her head back out into the corridor, silently counting off the doorways she had passed. She heard the footsteps of her pursuers pounding along the corridor and stepped back to hide among the deep shadows.

They ran past Tila and she shook her head as they charged past, then she sprang through the doorway and sprinted back the way she had come.

They heard her, tried to turn too quickly and crashed against a wall. They exchanged angry glances. One of them shoved himself away from the wall and gave chase. The other narrowed his eyes, swore, and followed, ignoring the bright new pain in his knee.

This time after Tila passed the junction she slapped each door as she ran by, counting again, looking for where she had made her mistake. Then she saw what she had missed. In the dim lighting was another hidden doorway. It was different to the others.

Most internal doors were constructed in the same way. An uninspired industrial design concerned only with utility and cost and nothing else; the sort of thing you would find on any starship. Yes, this was the door she was looking for. It was square and heavy with thick seals designed to withstand the vacuum of space.

She couldn't see any controls to the left or right of the door. That was unusual but not unheard of. Not every ship that had been absorbed by the Juggernaut was properly aligned, assuming you subscribed to any ideal about what the 'proper' way was to fuse one starship to another. Some scalpers just weren't fussy about the finished job. Others even preferred the odd layouts which resulted from disoriented ships.

Tila never understood the appeal. Who would want a floor to become a ceiling because one ship had been attached upside down? And at times like this it just made her life harder.

She looked above the door. There it was. She jumped up, slapped the single button with her palm and waited.

Nothing.

She tried again, one quick hammer stroke with the heel of her palm. A weak light flickered in the centre of the button and the door gave out a horrible shriek as if angry to be disturbed after all these years.

It opened eight inches and stopped.

Too small.

How close were the others? Tila cocked her head to listen for the oncoming footsteps.

Too close.

She pulled the metal bar from her back, and inserted it through the small gap. She tested it to make sure it was secure and then grabbed it with both hands. She pulled as hard has she could to lever the door open and hoped she was strong enough.

The door moved another inch.

Not enough.

This wasn't working, and the footsteps were coming closer.

She pulled the bar free and held it away from her body. Fingers squeezed it in just the right way and it sprung open to four times its original length with a sudden snap. Give me a lever long enough, she thought.

She tried again, the longer staff multiplying her efforts and the door opened a few more inches, but it still wasn't enough.

The two breathless men staggered around the corner at the end of the corridor. Too tired to shout anymore they stumbled toward her as fast as they could.

She was running out of time and she needed this door open.

Sometimes you have to pull, sometimes you have to push.

Tila swiftly pulled herself up and over the bar and braced her feet against the ceiling. She grunted with the effort, arms and legs straining against the corrosion of the years.

This time she felt something give. It was only a few more inches, but it was enough.

She dropped to the floor, tossed her staff through the doorway and pulled herself up by her fingertips. She wriggled through the opening which was now big enough, just, to admit her.

She crossed the threshold and fell. Not down, but sideways.

The intensity and sudden shift in where down was supposed to be caught her by surprise. Her shoulder crashed into the floor that a moment before had been a wall.

She picked up the staff and climbed to her feet. Looking back through the door which was now oriented correctly, she realised she should have expected this shift in the gravity shelf. Bulkhead doors don't open top to bottom. That should have been a clue.

Still, at least the floor wasn't the ceiling this time.

Tila looked away from the vertical slit in the bulkhead. The sight of the corridor outside at right angles to her floor was disorientating.

She rubbed her sore shoulder where it had taken the brunt of the impact and she squeezed the staff again in just the right place. It snapped back to its former length with a metallic sigh and a satisfying click.

The weak light from the corridor behind her was the only illumination Tila had. The first thing she noticed in was the low, dark shapes scattered throughout the dim room. The light knifed its way through the dusty air, barely enough to show her the storage lockers built into the far wall.

Shadows suddenly flashed through the light beam. Tila turned and saw the hands of her pursuers tugging at the bulkhead door in an effort open it wide enough for them to climb in. She heard one of them pick something up from the hallway and together they tried to force the opening wider.

They strained against the old door mechanism until their improvised tool snapped. Like the rest of the Juggernaut it was too old and worn to be of any real use. They resorted to brute strength instead, and little by little the opening grew wider.

Unhurried and unconcerned while they tired themselves out, Tila scanned the room. Her eyes adjusted quickly to the gloom, and the room was growing brighter by the second as the door behind her yielded inch by inch.

She saw now that the dim shapes scattered around the room were bed frames, now more rust than metal. If this was a bunk room then the bulkhead couldn't have been an airlock door after all, she thought.

At one time, something had breached the wall to her left. Messy repair work had made no effort to conceal the gaping hole in the wall. Something, maybe another ship, had ripped through the wall like a fist through a paper bag.

Micro-foam sealant decorated the wall in splashes of pink and blue. The bright pastel colours were too cheerful for this dingy apartment.

As Tila moved through the room she noticed something glinting on the wall to her right. A brass plaque. Years of grime had long since hidden the surface of the polished metal but a recent scratch had uncovered a sharp, bright line which winked at her in the darkness.

Tila stepped though the light beam and wiped away the worst of the dirt with her sleeve. It read in bold letters '*Eclipse*'. Underneath, in smaller text, it said 'Registered and licenced by Mirador Port Authority'.

Jackpot.

The bulkhead door finally crashed open and the room suddenly brightened. The men's shadows leered into the room like dusky ghosts.

One of them moved too quickly and in the darkness and his haste made the same mistake as Tila. He fell awkwardly, caught of balance by the shifting gravity plane and landed on his back.

The other cautiously rolled into the room, his feet aligned with the wall to his left. He cleared the lip of the door and neatly turned his feet to meet the oncoming wall.

The first man struggled to his feet, swearing and blaming the other for his mishap.

Tila considered her options. They had been following her for some time now, so it was unlikely she was escaping this without a fight. She could just give them what they wanted, but even that had its risks. In her experience men always wanted more than what was on offer.

She quickly tried to prise the brass plate from the wall but it was too firmly attached.

Typical, she thought. Everything else in this city falls apart if you so much as look at it wrong but this plaque had to be well-made.

Tila turned to face the two men. They had stopped bickering and were advancing, separating to approach her from the sides.

She stared them down, and held her ground. Defiant, yet ready to move.

"Que pasa?" she said cautiously. They didn't reply. "You can't have it," she told them.

"You don't even know what we want," said the one on the left. He was the handsome one, she decided, but it was a close call either way. He had fewer scars and most of his teeth.

"You know this isn't my first day, right?" said Tila.

"Maybe we want to give you something instead," said the other. He gestured obscenely with the only three fingers of his right hand.

Tila rolled her eyes. Amateurs.

Handsome pulled a knife. A short, broad blade with a hooked point. "Just give us the staff, and we'll let you go."

"Promise," lied the second man. His fingers still twitched.

Tila looked at the knife. Handsome held it properly, like a weapon and not a toy.

These men were more serious than she thought. Fine. Better to play it safe and live again another day. She held up a hand.

"Okay, okay." She reached over her shoulder with her other hand and pulled out the compact staff. "Here." She made as if to pass it to them, then dropped it. It clanged on the metal floor with an unusual sound and rolled forward to stop by their feet.

She held their gaze. "Oops," she said.

Handsome snapped his fingers at his companion and pointed at the staff, "Get it."

Tila fixed her eyes on Handsome. She had learned the hard way to never take her eyes off the man with the weapon. Fingers obviously thought the same, because his eyes were locked on Tila while his crippled hand scrabbled around on the floor. He found something, and with a triumphant smirk closed his hand over his companions foot.

Handsome glanced down.

Tila exploded.

In the half-second it took the men to react Tila slammed her knee into Fingers' face, then stamped on Handsome's foot, jabbed him in the face with her left to knock him off balance, and finished with a swift right-hook. Handsome hopped backward with yelp. On the back swing Tila brought her elbow down as hard as she could onto Finger's head.

Handsome shook his head and rushed back in, swinging wide with brute force and un-thinking rage. Tila turned her shoulder to meet him, grabbed his knife-hand and forced his arm painfully over her shoulder. She twisted his wrist the wrong way until she felt some-thing give. Handsome yelped in pain and dropped the knife fell from limp fingers and skittered away.

Now Tila was facing the plaque again. Keep-ing her tight grip on Handsome's wrist she lunged toward the wall and dropped to one knee, pulling Handsome with her. His head bounced off the brass plaque and he dropped.

Tila turned, ready for Fingers. He was on his feet again. He ignored the knife and instead held Tila's compact staff over one shoulder like a baton.

He charged, swinging high.

Tila went low. She dived between his legs and rolled, then kicked to her feet, knife in hand. Fingers yelled and swung again. Tila ducked and stabbed him in the foot, plunging the knife home. She felt the blade scrape on the metal floor. Fingers screamed, and dropped the staff.

He collapsed to the floor and struggled to pull the knife out, whimpering in pain.

Tila crouched, yanked the knife from his foot, and grabbed a fistful of hair to pull back his head.

"Don't...don't..," he pleaded.

"You'll live," she said, and slammed his head into the floor.

Tila wiped the blood from the knife on his filthy clothes and turned her attention back to the brass nameplate. There was a dent where she had introduced it to Handsome's skull. Not so handsome now.

Tila used her sleeve to wipe the dent clean and ran the knife around the edges of the seal. She took her time to cut it away, being careful not to nick the metal with the blade. It was the work of a few moments to loosen the plaque enough so that she could lever it free with the flat of the blade. It finally, reluctantly, came free from the wall with a satisfying pop. She secured the plaque in her bag and threw the knife into a dark corner of the room.

She saw Handsome was waking from his stupor. He saw the staff on the floor and chanced it, reaching for it with unsteady fingers. Tila stepped forward, putting her full weight on his hand. Fingers splayed beneath her boot and he gave up a pitiful cry as he tried to tug his hand free.

Without taking her eyes off him Tila nudged the staff out of his reach, then stamped down. Her toes clipped the staff and it skidded away. Backspin and momentum fought for the upper hand. Backspin won. The staff slowed, hesitated and rolled back to her. Tila bounced it onto her foot and flicked her leg sideways. The staff hooked between her ankle and knee and spun up to eye level. She caught it with one hand and slotted it home under her backpack.

The she stepped over Handsome and headed for the door.

Handsome pulled himself to his knees, clutched his broken fingers and spat at her. "Next time we see you we'll kill you."

"I hear that a lot," said Tila as she adjusted her pack for comfort and started toward the doorway, "But next time I'll still let you live."

Confusion overcame anger. "Why?"

"Because life hurts more," she said.

3

Ellie huffed on the visor of her helmet and gave it one last vigorous rub with her sleeve. After a final critical examination, she was satisfied.

She pulled it on, tucked blond hair behind her ears, and heard the magnetic latches click into place. She squeezed her eyes shut and swallowed to stave off the discomfort caused by the change in air pressure. It never worked. Her ears still popped, but Ellie was ever the optimist.

She wiggled into her seat and tapped a button on the reconditioned control panel to open the channel to Malachi, but he was already speaking.

"...Easy on the bend."

"Huh? Say again?" Ellie's muscle memory took over and ran through the pre-flight sequence on autopilot. Fingers flicked switches and pressed buttons while her mind concentrated on what Malachi was saying.

"I said, you can go for it on the straight but take it easy on the bend. Your ship can't handle those tight turns."

Ellie's little racer hummed around her as the flight systems sprang to life. Pre-igniters rumbled behind her, firing up the engine core. The vibrations made her seat shudder.

"It has before."

"When?"

"Last week. Anything else I should know?"

"You should be able to beat him off the line but his engine is going to give him a greater top speed. And we didn't have a race last week."

"Maybe we did?"

"*We* did not, Ellie. You know you shouldn't race without me."

"Oh Malachi, you sound just like your dad when you worry."

Ellie felt a change in the vibrations rumbling through her seat, and the pitch of the engine whine increased. The pre-ignition sequence was over.

She entered the next command without looking. Full power was moments away.

Malachi said nothing. Ellie knew he would be trying to work out if she had just insulted him. In her opinion he needed to relax more. He over-analysed everything. It was a quality which made him a wonderful engineer and valuable race technician, but it made for lousy conversation if she ever compared him to his father.

The computer chirped once to tell Ellie the ship was ready to launch. It was her favourite sound.

Through the cockpit she watched today's opponent, Santini, running through his own launch sequence. He glanced back at her. She waved and gave him a friendly thumbs-up. Santini ignored her, pulled on his own helmet, and launched.

"Rude," Ellie muttered to herself. She took the controls, released her ship from the deck, rose above it and followed him through the bay doors of the Juggernaut and out into space.

There were other ships already outside. Eager observers waited just beyond the bay doors, ready to chase the two ships around the course and get the best possible view of the action.

Eight hundred metres away four ships hovered over the surface of the city in a square.

They hovered perpendicular to the Juggernaut's hull and marked the start and finish line of the race.

For the people who had become known as the dispossessed: the refugees, the criminals and the homeless, the Juggernaut was at worst a prison, and at best a bitter reminder that somewhere out there, somewhere else among the Commonwealth planets, was a world they had once called home. Ellie was too young to remember a life before the Juggernaut, and since being orphaned during a raid six years ago, she had no chance at another home.

Almost everyone dreamed of escape but few people ever left. Even if they were fortunate enough to have a ship capable of Jumping to another system they were unlikely to be able to afford the transit fees.

Most of the city operated on a barter system. Honest work that paid in hard currency was rare and was almost certainly not going to be lucrative enough to fund a new life elsewhere in the Commonwealth.

If someone had the money and a ship it had probably been obtained through illicit channels. That meant a bounty, and that meant they were going to be picked up within hours of arriving in one of the neighbouring, and law-abiding, systems.

Bounty hunters rarely followed their leads back to the Juggernaut. The Celato system was lawless and crawling with pirates, so only the highest value marks were chased into the city. Anything less wasn't good business.

And if they were that rare citizen with honest credit and the means to travel then something else was keeping them here. Something so terrible that it made life on the Juggernaut, far from the civilised worlds of the Commonwealth, their best option.

But none of these applied to Ellie. She had committed no crime, she simply had no desire to leave. The city was home.

It was also her playground.

If you dared to enter and could salvage, repair or build something space worthy, you could race.

Like anything dangerous, the youth had quickly made it their own. The teenagers of the disparate Juggernaut communities had organised themselves well enough to hold races whenever and wherever they liked.

With almost a million people on board there was always someone, somewhere, ready to race. The ever-changing surface of the Juggernaut made for an unpredictable course and the lack of any effective authority within the city or the star system meant that there was no one to stop them. Racing was almost a rite of passage in some communities but one truth of life aboard the Juggernaut was universal: There was nowhere else to go.

No matter how fast you went, you couldn't escape the city.

Malachi couldn't escape the crowd.

He elbowed his way to the window of the viewing platform and rechecked the video feed coming through to his data pad.

The viewing platform for this race was the grimy bridge of an old private yacht. In its day, it had been a valuable ship. Now its spacious bridge was filled with laughing teenagers. Its elegant lines were lost to ugly but serviceable welds. The beautiful ship was now just another part of the city.

The *Mandalay* had at least been attached right side up, relatively speaking, so the bridge windows commanded a perfect view of square that was to be the start and finish of the race. Malachi could see Ellie coasting into position.

Half the crowd were eager to see her win again, half of them were looking forward to seeing her lose, and all of them were in his way.

This race was to be a single lap around the underside of the city so most of it would be out of the line of sight of the spectators.

Instead, video feeds transmitted by ships holding position along the course and by pursuit craft would ensure no detail of the action would be missed.

The video feeds were for the benefit of the audience but Malachi and Ellie found them invaluable. While Ellie gave her full attention to the next hundred metres of the course, Malachi studied her opponents and advised her on what to do.

It seemed an obvious solution to them and they didn't understand why no one else did what they did.

Tila tried explaining to them once that it was a matter of pride. That pilots lived the role of the hero, that they loved to fight off all challengers with nothing but their skill and their wits. Every other racer wanted the glory for themselves.

Tila said teamwork was just an excuse for someone to let you down but in their case she couldn't deny that it worked.

Malachi and Ellie had dismissed her opinion on the grounds that she was nothing special in the cockpit and certainly no racer. So how could she understand pilots? But Tila did understand pride. Most racers were too arrogant and too proud to work with anyone else.

Too arrogant until they met Ellie, anyway.

Her win record spoke for itself, and Ellie's growing reputation was a small, blond microcosm of the change in fortunes for the New Haven community.

When Malachi and his father Theodore arrived in New Haven no one wanted to build a racer. It was the furthest thing from anyone's mind. At the time, the community did not even have reliable air and water. Theo had repaired and reconditioned the life support systems and he had taken the time to train others. As he passed on his skills he was able to take on bigger challenges. Eventually Theo restored the New Haven space dock. It was the only real asset New Haven owned, and it was the one thing which had attracted him to this community in the first place.

Once the dock was operational New Haven was open for business. Malachi and his father began repairing and servicing ships. This brought them a valuable income, and a ready supply of spare parts, some of which were even now hovering over the starting line.

But every silver lining has a cloud. Their rising star brought to New Haven the unwelcome attention of the gangs which preyed on the weaker communities. The gangs which had killed Ellie's adopted parents.

Malachi reflected that somehow, Ellie at seventeen seemed younger and more helpless than Tila did at fourteen, six years ago. Even back then, Tila was a fighter, and she had put her ferocious skills to use defending Ellie from raiders which had breached the New Haven perimeter.

If Tila had not been there to saver her that day Ellie might never have got the chance to fly.

Malachi flicked through different camera angles on his data pad and smiled to himself at the thought of the two Ellies he knew. In the cockpit, she was tenacious and unyielding, but out of the cockpit she floated through life carefree and effortless in her own blonde bubble. And like a bubble she was about as useful and as dangerous.

Tila on the other hand, was never going to make a name for herself as a pilot, but on foot she personified athletic grace and a practical, ruthless efficiency.

Between them stood Malachi: thoughtful, careful and wary of any outcome that did not confirm to the engineered specifications. They teased him for his caution but he reminded them, often, that someone had to think about the consequences.

His data pad beeped and the surrounding crowd began chanting a countdown. The race was starting.

Both ships accelerated hard. As soon as they passed the start line they dived low to skim the Juggernaut's surface as close as they dared.

This winner of this race would be the first one to complete a loop under the city. Speed and nerves were needed to win. The closer they flew to the surface the shorter their route would be, but the risk was greater. It was a dangerous combination. A perfect test of speed and skill.

At least it's not a core run, Malachi thought. That takes a special kind of crazy.

Core runs were theoretical races that took ships through the heart of the city, from one end to the other. They were rumoured to be possible but no one Malachi knew had ever even attempted one, let alone completed one. The Juggernaut was a haphazard construction of a thousand different ships, so it made sense there would be voids and openings all over the surface. Maybe somewhere there was a hidden entrance to the maze of tunnels within, but as far as Malachi could tell they were just convenient holes in which to plug the next derelict hulk.

Many would-be adventurers had explored as far as they dared but their stories all ended the same way. Sooner or later - usually sooner - they found a wall of metal barring their way, or the openings were just too small to allow their ships to pass.

Some obstacles were far more deadly. Venting gas, radiation leaks and the risk of structural collapse were just some of the dangers waiting in the dark.

Malachi had also noticed how the stories he heard always became more exciting with each retelling.

If a route through the city were found it would be an incredible race - perfect for a thrill seeker like Ellie Young, but far too risky for Malachi Chambers.

You lose one hundred percent of the races you don't survive, he told her. Of all the advice she ignored, at least she listened to *that*. Ellie might be dangerous when she was in her little ship, he thought, but she wasn't stupid.

The ships were already out of sight of the *Mandalay's* bridge so the spectators switched their attention to the video feeds on screens and personal datapads.

Ellie was already in the lead, although nudging ahead of her opponent by only a half-length.

Both ships were already dangerously close to the surface. They crept lower still. With only two metres to spare they skimmed the top of one of the communications hubs which littered the surface of the city. More radio towers, satellite dishes and countless other protrusions threatened to reach up and snatch the ships from their course as they streaked overhead.

They reached the first edge of the city and dived over. Santini turned faster and made up the ground he had lost on the straight. Ellie growled her annoyance into Malachi's ear as he looked on, helpless.

The crowd cheered again, lapping up the drama. It seemed to Malachi that the crowd had split their affection right down the middle.

Wagers were placed, deals were struck, and Malachi dug the fingernails of his right hand into his palm while the other hand gripped the datapad even more tightly.

Ellie zipped around the lower edge of the city and she and Santini twisted a half-turn to reorient themselves as she swooped around the city rim.

Now the city was above them, and the emptiness of space below.

Santini pulled further ahead. Although she had the greater acceleration his tighter, smaller turn had given him the edge he needed. And he had the greater top speed so the straight run to the far edge of the under-city meant Ellie's chances of catching him were small.

But Santini wasn't leaving this race to chance. His ship suddenly swung through Ellie's line. Ellie saw it in time pulled away to avoid a collision and was forced to dive for the safety of open space.

Malachi tapped the commlink, toggling the option to leave it open. "What was that?! You ok?"

"Yes," said Ellie through clenched teeth. What Santini had done wasn't cheating because there were no rules.

Her opponent wasted no time in capitalizing on Ellie's misfortune. While she powered up through the curve to get back on her racing line back Santini had increased the distance between them and was now fast approaching the next turn.

"How are you-" Malachi began.

"I got it," said Ellie.

"But what are you...,"

Ellie cut Malachi off through clenched teeth. "I got it!"

Malachi flicked through every camera view available on his datapad. His mind formulated and discarded a dozen options for Ellie but there was nothing he could do.

Now comfortably in the lead, Santini was arcing through a safe, gentle curve around the underside of the Juggernaut. He knew there were no safe shorter routes.

What he didn't know was how flexible Ellie's definition of 'safe' was when victory was on the line. Malachi had a sickening feeling that he knew what Ellie was about to do.

Edging the rim of the city was a crash zone. Usually old spaceships were layered on to the city, or used to fill gaps. At crash zones ships had simply been rammed bow-first into the city, leaving sterns their hulls and engines sticking out from the surface. Cross bracing among the hulls provided additional strength and reduced the risk of collapse.

Flying through the crash zone on a level surface would be like a fly trying to thread its way between a dozen webs. Flying through a crash zone on a turn meant the pilot would be unable to see what was coming until it was too late. It would dramatically reduce the distance around the edge of the city, but it was the insane choice.

Naturally it was what Ellie was going to do.

"Ellie, no!" warned Malachi.

"You're distracting me."

"Good! So stop!"

"Can't."

"Can't?"

"Won't."

Santini began the long, safe route over the zone in a smooth curve designed to take him safely around the dangerous turn and ease him to the upper surface of the city and the home straight.

Ellie looked up at the gun metal grey towers overhead, spun her ship one hundred eighty degrees so they were below, and dived in.

A murmur rippled through the crowd surrounding Malachi.

Oh no, thought Malachi. *Not again.*

Ellie inched her ship closer to the unyielding wall of the city and urged it on with whispered pleading. "Comeon, comeon, comeon, comeon."

Santini had already reached the top of his climb and was levelling out for the final dash to the finish line.

The crash zone sprawled across the surface of the hull before her, filling her horizon with giant pillars of steel.

The crowd was chanting now, a chorus growing in volume. "Closer. Closer. Closer. Closer."

Malachi was afraid to watch and afraid to look away. He always hated this part.

Ellie dived into the crash zone. She twisted and turned her ship as it raced between the obstacles which towered over her. The race course was gone. Now everything was the next half-second, then the next, then the next. She flew on instinct and reflexes alone. She risked a glance up. Santini flew above the zone, high and safe.

But she was making up ground.

Ellie jinked and dodged her ship through the rest of the zone. The centrifugal force generated by the turn threatened to tear Ellie from her seat. Her body strained against the buckles that held her tight.

And then she was clear.

Ellie gritted her teeth against the forces trying to throw her from her ship and shoved her flight stick forward. Her little craft plunged down once more to meet the city. The surface fell away beneath her and she crested the horizon to enter the final straight.

Santini had the luxury of time on his side. He had completed his careful arc and was levelling out before completing his final approach.

Ellie was still climbing.

"I can't turn fast enough," Ellie cried as she wrestled her ship out of its climb and back into a dive. "He's getting away. I need more power!"

Malachi's mind raced. Technically she needed more thrust. But the only other thrusters on the ship were the landing thrusters in the underbelly and nose and they were on the wrong side of the ship. Useless.

Schematics and diagrams flashed through his mind's eye, examining the options, considering the variables. Santini was faster. Ellie had closed the gap but her vector was all wrong, and she couldn't change it fast enough.

Then he blinked.

Problem solved.

"Invert!" he shouted. The people around him jumped.

"What?"

"Invert your ship! Use your landing thrusters!"

Ellie gave no reply but Malachi was still watching the screens. He saw her ship roll over in a quick half-turn. Landing thrusters designed for a careful, controlled landing ignited at full power. The nose of the ship kicked hard against the stars and aimed for the finish line.

Malachi checked the flight telemetry on his datapad. The displays showed the race, but in his hand was every other bit of data he needed, including the projected vectors of the two ships.

Santini, of course, was heading straight for the finish line. He had an easy run, free and clear. Ellie was coming in fast but not fast enough. It was going to be close, and she wasn't going to win. A draw was the best she could hope for now.

"Ellie, you've pulled it back. Just keep going and you have a draw."

"A draw?" She sounded disgusted at the very idea. "I might as well lose!"

"Ellie, this guy is good. A draw is a good result."

"I don't want to draw."

"But you can't win."

"Don't tell me what to do!"

The vector on his datapad shifted again.

"Ellie, you overdid it on the landing thrusters."

"No, I didn't."

"You're coming in too steep. You're going to miss the line."

"No, I'm not."

"Ellie, you're going to hit him!"

"I'm going to win."

Ellie held her line.

Safety mechanisms disagreed. Collision warnings sounded throughout her cockpit. Red lights rippled across control panels. She knew her opponent heard it too, and he would have to make a choice: continue to the finish and risk crashing or turn aside, avoid a crash but miss the line.

With seconds to go the alarms began to crescendo.

Ellie held her line.

Her engines screamed with effort as she closed the distance to her target.

Santini held steady, willing to risk the crash, daring her to pull up.

The space between the ships vanished.

Two hundred metres.

One hundred metres.

Fifty metres.

Ellie held her line.

Ellie's klaxon blared its urgent message. Warning lights danced in front of her, desperate for attention, but she held her nerve.

She stayed the line.

Santini was dead ahead now. Before them both was the finish. The collision was imminent. Everything around and within Ellie told her to pull up or slow down, but she didn't like to lose.

Ellie held her line.

Santini broke. His ship dived and turned wide of the line. Ellie blasted through it.

"Wooooooo!"

"Yes!" said Malachi, punching the air.

The crowd around him cheered and whooped, thrilled by the outrageous spectacle they had just seen.

"I don't think you will be able to do that again next time, Ellie."

"Next time I won't have to. I need a faster ship, Mal."

Malachi could hear her grinning despite the complaint. "I'll see what I can do the next time I get some parts."

"Great! Also, I need to make tighter turns so maybe you can reduce the weight or something? And a better flight suit. The seat feels too hard when I'm accelerating, and-"

Malachi cut her off. "How about the collision warning? Anything wrong with that?"

A pause.

"No. That seems to be ok."

Malachi rolled his eyes. "Anything else?"

"The air smells funny in here. Can you fix that?"

"You treat me like I'm your personal slave technician."

"No, I treat you like a big brother."
He laughed. She was right. He did look at her like a little sister.

Ellie had really been adopted by the entire community of New Haven. There were few people in the city who could resist Ellie's natural optimism. If they were given the choice almost everyone would choose Ellie over the other orphan girl in their midst. Tila was capable and resourceful, but Ellie could light up a room by walking through the door.

To Ellie, family was something far greater than the two people who brought you into the world. They were what made you feel part of it. They were the people who made it a world worth living in and belonging to, even here on the Juggernaut.

Even though Malachi had known her for years Ellie still seemed young. He had to remind himself that even though she easily fell into the role the helpless little sister Ellie was older and wiser than she sometimes appeared.

Malachi thought again of the race he had just witnessed.

Perhaps not.

4

Councilman Theodore Chambers made his excuses and broke away from the small group of well-wishers, and his own birthday party, to look for his son.

He guessed what was holding Malachi up. The problem would be that girl again. She was a rogue element in a fragile society. Theo sympathised with her predicament but held firm to his conviction. He could not afford to give her any special treatment. Since he had been welcomed to the New Haven council he was responsible for the lives of almost a thousand citizens. All of whom needed to be fed and protected from the dangers of the Juggernaut, both inside and out.

Tila Vasquez was not so special that her need to roam free could be allowed to threaten the security of everyone else.

Theo bumped into a young, excitable couple as stepped through the airlock which was stuck open by rust and decay, on their way to the party. He smiled at them and made small talk for a few minutes and was under no illusion that their excitement stemmed from the fact it was his birthday.

The renovations of the decommissioned livestock transport ship, registration BV601, had recently been completed, and Theo's fiftieth birthday had provided the excuse for the community to celebrate. It was more than welcome after such a successful project.

Theo's original aim had been to simply make this space habitable for their growing population. The fact that he had personally trained four new engineers in the basics of life support technologies was the proverbial icing on the proverbial cake.

The couple pattered off the polite small talk expected of people who wanted to be on their way but didn't want to seem rude, as Theo tried and failed to remember their names. Eventually he shook the husband's hand, accepted a kiss on the cheek from the wife and told them to go have a good time. He watched them leave and smiled at their happy union.

He was glad they had found each other, especially here, but he was not surprised. Love, like any other seed, could take root in the darkness.

The couple joined hands as they walked. The husband whispered something in her ear and she giggled and playfully slapped his shoulder.

Why couldn't Malachi find someone like that, Theo wondered. *Why couldn't I find that again?*

Theo adored his son but still found him to be a frustrating young man. Even Malachi would admit to that. But Theo recognised his son's strengths too. Malachi was more than capable of dealing with the finances and clients of the little business they had carved out for themselves here, but his real gift was understanding the machines they dealt with daily, and knowing how to fix them.

Theo smiled to himself again. He was a good engineer, his years of study and alphabet soup of qualifications could attest to that, but Malachi had an easy gift with machines. All you had to do was explain what a machine was supposed to do, then hand him a manual and a box of tools, and wait.

Maybe it was the natural consequence of how he had raised his son. Malachi's mother, Theo's wife, had not been in Malachi's life - either of their lives - long enough. Malachi was only six when they arrived on the Juggernaut twelve years earlier. He was nine when his mother died in the raid. Theo had worked every hour he could so they could survive, and so young Malachi had spent his childhood in the workshop, helping his over-protective father with anything he could and absorbing, totally, everything he was taught. Malachi had a mind like a bucket. He was fortunate to have a father with a mind like a tap.

Before his family had moved to the Freeport of New Haven, Theo had worked as chief engineer for one of the interstellar corporations on a range of projects from experimental engines (promising) to asteroid-based arcologies (too expensive) and from space elevators (too theoretical) to moon-based launch systems (efficient but already outdated).

Their family had ended up here for the same reason everyone did - they had nowhere else to go. The Juggernaut was their best, last and safest option. And besides, no one searches the trash for treasure.

One day soon Theo planned to explain to Malachi why and how they had ended up here, but he suspected Malachi had already pieced together enough clues and overheard enough whispered conversations of past regret to learn the truth. A business deal gone bad had brought them to the brink of bankruptcy.

The ensuing court cases had done the rest.

With no money left to prove himself innocent Theo had sold the last of their possessions and ran. They raised enough money for one last journey. One final destination. The Juggernaut.

No central authority existed in the Celato system so Theo couldn't be extradited if someone came looking. After all, someone needed to sign the paperwork.

But this didn't mean they were completely safe. His creditors, or the bounty hunters they hired, still wanted him, but the cost and risk of seeking out one man in a lawless star system, aboard a dangerous labyrinthine city of almost a million people meant that he was unlikely to be found even if someone thought the effort to be worth their while.

The dangers of the present had protected them from the dangers of the past. There was one advantage to being a member of the dispossessed after all.

A mixed blessing if ever there was one, thought Theo.

Once they had settled into life on board Theo soon discovered his skills were in demand in every area of city life. Life support, water reclamation, hydroponics, heating, and lighting.

With the benefit of his expert knowledge, New Haven had thrived as new immigrants and migrants from elsewhere in the city came to stay.

Despite the added strain on every available resource slowly, gradually, and carefully, Theo and his son transformed one small corner of the Juggernaut into an area where people could at last not just survive, but actually live.

Since then Malachi had grown up in something of a bubble, constantly discouraged from taking risks by his father. Theo knew he could often be an overbearing and overprotective parent but Malachi never complained, at least not to him. Maybe his son only endured it because he loved his father.

Two young boys rounded the corner carrying a heavy pot between them. They wobbled, and Theo made to intervene, but then they recovered, hefted the pot a little higher and carried on. Behind them followed their mother, Theo assumed.

She trailed behind them just a little way, just enough to let them feel independent, but Theo could see the fear etched into her brow that the food they carried might not make it to the party.

"It's just potatoes," she apologised she passed, as if this would make everything alright if the boys did end up spilling the food.

Of course it was potatoes. Only mushrooms grew better here. Mushrooms and rats. And nobody wanted to eat rat at a party.

Was it too much to ask for more than this on a man's fiftieth birthday, he wondered. He chided himself for his selfish thought. This wasn't about his birthday, or the celebration of a ship restored. Everyone deserved better than this life, even his only son. No, especially his only son.

And yet Malachi never complained. On the surface, he seemed content with his life of technical problems which he rarely failed to solve. He didn't waste time dreaming of escape and adventure and romance. He was too practical for that.

Besides, adventures, of a sort, were never far away on the Juggernaut. Not if you counted the roaming gangs, local warlords, the raiders and pirates, and the frequent attacks and constant attempted thefts of their water and power. If you really wanted adventure it was there for the taking, just like everything else in the city.

Theo was grateful his son was more interested in helping a customer and keeping the workshop organised than he was in escaping the Juggernaut on some foolish crusade.

It never occurred to Theo that a complete lack of options might have had something to do with it.

The truth was that his son had no way to leave. Very few did once they were here. Theo owned just one ship, and even this had taken a year of work and restoration to make spaceworthy again. There was nothing new on the Juggernaut. Nothing new under their dying sun.

If you couldn't repair, remodel or recondition it then you didn't get to use it. Sure, there were plenty of short-range craft around. Runabouts and racers were perfectly adequate for the short hops to other communities and free ports, but Theo's ship was one of the few vessels capable of a system Jump. That made it priceless.

The *Rhino* was certainly nothing special to look at but it was big enough to function as a mobile workshop which made it ideal for those awkward jobs in situ. It was also spacious enough to transport larger items, like engines, back to his workshop for repair. Without the *Rhino*, Theo would never have been able to source and supply the items New Haven needed to transform itself from a community that was barely surviving to one which had almost – almost - begun to prosper.

Ships capable of any sort of extended journey were incredibly rare on the Juggernaut, and therefore incredibly valuable. And ships capable of making a system Jump was almost unheard of.

Typically, the only way out of the Celato system was to buy passage alongside a Jump surrogate, and that was expensive. Theo was sometimes able to scrape together enough money to buy passage on an outbound Jump out if he needed something from one of their three neighbours, but he also had to make sure he had enough money for the return trip. He avoided spending more than a day or two away from the Celato system. The risk of being seen was too high.

It had been months since Theo had needed to leave the Juggernaut for supplies of any kind, but thanks to a recent deal he had made to repair the drive of a cargo ship which had broken down while in transit between the Celato Beacons, he would shortly have the funds.

It was any irony Theo didn't appreciate that even though he was one of the few people in the city with the means to leave the system he could never be away for long. Sooner or later his ship would flag up on some watch list and he would have to return before someone tried to arrest him or cash in a standing warrant.

The sound of approaching footsteps brought him back to the moment. They were light, bright steps which tapped quickly upon the cold floor. Theo recognised them. He smiled to himself and retreated into the shadows. He liked to play the stern overseer on occasion.

Ellie skipped around the corner and suddenly a large and imposing figure stepped out of the shadows to bar her way. Recessed lights reflected off the dark skin of his bald head. His muscled arms were folded across his broad chest. He looked down at her, his face impossible to read behind the cropped salt-and-pepper beard. He filled the corridor and loomed over her. Ellie might have found the man intimidating if she had not known him so well.

"Eleanor Young!" boomed Theo, more statement than question.

Ellie made a face. She hated that name. It sounded so grown up.

"You're late," he continued.

"I'm sorry," said Ellie. She wasn't.

"And where, young lady, is my wayward son?"

"Malachi's right behind me. Tila's coming too. She might already be here. Have you seen her?"

Theo ignored this last question. "You have some good news for me at least, I hope?"

"Maybe. If you let me in," she teased.

Theo frowned and bent down to bring his face level with Ellie's.

"And why should I do a thing like that?" he dared her.

"Because this," said Ellie, and kissed him on the cheek, "Happy birthday, Theo."

"Ha!" roared Theo as he swept Ellie up in a bear hug as he spun around. Ellie laughed until the bear hug made breathing too painful. She patted his arms in submission until he put her down. When she was back on solid ground she took a moment to smooth out her clothes, then she looked up at him and said, "Ow."

He winked. "If I thought for one moment you didn't like that I wouldn't do it."

"Yes, you would," she accused him playfully, "But I don't have time to argue today. I need to find Tila."

"Ellie," he called after her as she started to turn the corner. Her head popped back out, "Did you at least win?"

Ellie just grinned and vanished.

Theo hovered for another minute waiting for his son to appear but it seemed Malachi had been delayed longer than Ellie expected. Perhaps he should return to the town square? It would be a shame to miss out on his own birthday party, even despite the food.

He loved Ellie like a daughter. Everyone did. But the comparisons with Tila were inevitable considering how much time they spent together.

The girls had become close friends the day Tila saved Ellie's life. Ellie was just eleven when the raiders attacked New Haven. Tila was only fourteen. Theo remembered that day almost too well. He and Ellie both lost something precious.

Perhaps Tila had too. No one should have to fight for their life at fourteen, and no fourteen-year old girl should have to take one.

Ellie had followed Tila around like a puppy for weeks after that. Who could blame her? Tila made her feel safe.

Tila had shown her mettle that day. Theo could respect her courage and admire her strength but it was a pity she saw him as an enemy too.

But Theo also knew that Tila was too independent, too wilful. To put it plainly, she was too selfish. Theo worried about the influence she had on other members of the community, not least his own son.

Theo respected Tila's ideals of independence and freedom but had tried explaining to her that the price of living in a community was that sometimes individual rights had to suffer for the rights of the group.

A community, by definition, was a gathering of interdependent people. They relied upon each other. Tila had learned to rely only on herself.

If he was in a gracious mood Theo could admit there was a certain kind of nobility to her selfishness, and in another time and place he would support her completely, but they lived here and now and stability and structure and rules were what New Haven needed if it was to continue to grow in safety. Tila didn't seem to believe in rules. At least, not his rules.

By contrast Ellie was little more than inoffensive charm with golden hair. She was a good influence on Malachi. Tila was not. Ellie was sweetness and laughter. Tila brooded. Ellie welcomed people and was eager to make friends. Tila glowered and kept to herself. Ellie would tightly weave each person she met into the tapestry of her life. Tila built walls to keep them out.

In many ways, Ellie was still the puppy. Tila was the wolf.

Perhaps it would always be that way.

Malachi still hadn't appeared and Theo was getting hungry. He sighed and decided he had waited long enough. He turned on his heel, marched back into his party and tried to cast aside, for a few hours at least, the loss of the past, the fears of the present and the burden of authority and fatherhood.

And besides, maybe there would be a cake.

The crowds had grown noticeably larger in the few minutes since Theo had left and returned. A small part of him was pleased. It was edifying to think that everyone had turned out especially for him even though the dearth of celebrations meant that any communal event was well-attended.

Theo pushed through the thickening crowds and exchanged pleasantries and handshakes.

Elsewhere, Ellie was still hunting for her friend, certain this task, like everything else in her life, would be easier if she were only a little taller.

A hand suddenly grabbed her around the arm and pulled her to the side of the thoroughfare. Ellie shrieked in surprise.

"Hey," said Tila.

"You made me jump!"

Tila dismissed Ellie's complaint with a wave of her hand. "Oh, you jump at everything. I've never known anyone so fragile. So?"

"So what?"

"Did you win?"

"Always! What about you? Did you find it?"

Tila nodded and opened her bag just enough for Ellie alone to see inside. "Do you think he will like it?"

"Tila, he will love it!" she squealed. "It was very sweet of you to think of looking for that. Did you have any trouble?"

"Some. But they won't be bothering me again anytime soon."

Ellie gasped. "You didn't!"

"Of course not!" Tila snapped too quickly. "I'll never do that again. They'll be ok, just uncomfortable for a while. I don't go looking for trouble, you know."

Ellie raised a dubious eyebrow at this statement.

"I don't!" Tila protested again, "It just finds me."

"What finds you, Tila?" boomed Theo from behind them.

Tila, guilt etched on her face quickly spun around slapping the bag shut so Theo couldn't see what was inside. Ellie, like always, looked innocent of everything.

"Nothing," they chorused. Ellie grinned.

"There's no need to look so guilty," said Theo, as he searched their faces and wondered what Tila was hiding this time. "Where have you been? You know more hands around here would have made the work easier."

The unnecessary criticism riled Tila.

Theo said, "Ellie has been racing again, despite my concerns. And what about you Tila, have you been staying out of trouble?"

He was trying to sound jovial, Tila knew, but she heard the edge in his voice even if he didn't mean to put it there. She heard his criticism about work and trouble and it sparked rebellion within her. His light words sounded forced, as if he knew what her answer would be. As if he was being gracious enough to allow her the opportunity to not disappoint him this time. And Tila so often disappointed him.

But she worked hard and willingly when there was a real need. She just didn't consider party planning suited to her skills and she resented the way Theo seemed to give Ellie a free pass for racing. Everyone know how dangerous that was. So why did it seem like Theo, along with everyone else in New Haven, always questioned or challenged her actions just because she valued her independence.

So she told him the truth.

"I went to the *Eclipse.*"

Theo's face fell. "You went where? Tila! The pressure seals to that ship are well past their rated lifetime and I haven't authorised any checks on their integrity yet. You could have caused an explosive decompression and..." His expression hardened. "How could you be so...so stupid?"

"Stupid?" said Tila, her voice rising.

"Yes! Stupid! And thoughtless, and-"

"I've been down there a hundred times and I..." She stopped, suddenly aware of the hole she was digging. She could almost feel the temperature drop as she looked at Theo.

"You have been there more than once?" Theo said quietly.

"It was safe. I-"

"Tila, you have never committed fully to this community so what you choose to do is your own business, but you know that going to these areas risks exposing us to all manner of dangers, like pressure loss, or contaminated air, and I cannot allow that!"

"I-," Tila tried to say.

And what of the boundary defences we have in place? What if a raiding party found you, or followed you back?"

"Oh come on, Theo! This isn't about your defences. The air down there is fine. You did the work yourself and Malachi checked it for me." Tila was too caught up in her speech now to notice Theo bristled at the suggestion that Malachi had been with her. "You just don't want me making you look bad now you are on the council. You don't want anyone, least of all me, defying your rules. You don't want anyone to know more about this place than you do!"

Ellie touched Tila's arm softly.

"Tila..." she began but Tila angrily brushed Ellie's arm away and continued her tirade.

"You've done good things here, I'm not denying that, but you can't tell people what to do all the time. You can't just lock the doors, tell everyone they are safe and expect them to sit around and meekly comply with your orders."

Theo shouted back, "I do not 'give orders', Tila. The council does not give orders. We work to protect everyone in here from the dangers out there. Dangers you, of all people, should appreciate. And the rules are not mine. They exist to protect everyone here, yes, even you! We face daily threats from raiders and pirates and gangs from all over the Juggernaut, all over this system, and the more New Haven becomes known as a place of safety and God willing, prosperity, these dangers will continue to grow. So I will not allow your recklessness to endanger everyone else in this community! There are too many lives at stake here for your selfish whims to risk compromising."

"We haven't faced raiders in months!"

"And why do you think that is, Tila? Is it because of you? Is it because you are out there, thinking only of yourself, fighting to save us all? Or is it because the council works so hard to make allies of the other communities and free ports? A lone wolf cannot protect a pack, Tila. By acting as you do you are a liability to New Haven, and your selfishness..."

"Selfishness?! I'm the one who found the breach in the perimeter two months ago. I'm the one who told you someone was selling our perimeter ID codes!"

"Codes they would not have access to if they were not being so frequently used without authorisation!"

Tila yelled, "I don't need your authorisation! You are not my leader. You are not in charge of me. You're not my father!"

By now their raised voices had carried their fight to half the people in the town square, and Tila's final words rang throughout the high-ceilinged chamber. For one interminably long moment Tila and Theo glared at each other in a noiseless bubble, until somewhere a foot scraped on the floor, someone coughed, and the background noise of a dozen conversations began to wash over the sudden and uncomfortable silence.

Theo composed himself while Tila stood defiant before him, her fists clenched and muscles tense. He spoke again, calmly now, and more gentle. "Tila, believe me, I understand how you feel about this. Nobody is trying to impose limits on your freedom, but you must understand that these selfish actions put us all in danger, and no good can come of them."

Tila replied also in a lowered voice, but where Theo sounded gentle, Tila sounded bitter and betrayed. "I wasn't thinking of me," she said. Then she shoved her bag into Ellie's hands and marched away.

Ellie looked down at the bag with sadness. It had fallen open again under Tila's rough handling. Ellie closed it again and offered it to

Theo, who was looking at the floor and sighing angrily.

"This is for you, Theo." she said.

"What is this? A birthday present, from you?" His face softened a little.

"From Tila," said Ellie. "She hoped you would like it."

Intrigued by the gift and yet half-reluctant to discover what Tila might have gotten him, Theo opened the package and pulled out the brass nameplate of the ship which had delivered him, his wife and his son to the Juggernaut.

"What is it?" Theo asked.

"Gratitude," said Ellie, sadly. "And selflessness."

5

Tila folded her arms around the guardrail and worked her chin back and forth against wrists. The cold metal burned against her bare forearms as she let her mind empty and her legs swing free, and she stared unseeing into the mid-distance.

The noise and activity of the marketplace below her failed to penetrate the bubble of isolation had willed around herself.

The market was unusually busy today. Traders and merchants mingled with the residents of the New Haven freeport as well as visitors from neighbouring communities.

New arrivals trickled into the market from the nearby docks. Travel by ship was the safest option. Everyone else had to make the journey between the communities on foot. They would have moved in larger groups for safety, but once you were outside the secure New Haven perimeter the tunnels and corridors were still dangerous.

Tila heard and ignored the approaching footsteps. Not many of the people she knew would take the time to seek her out here, perched high above the market. She suspected she wasn't worth the trouble, not unless she was *in* trouble. She only knew two people who would bother, and the footsteps were too heavy for Ellie.

"Hey," she said when Malachi was close enough. It was just a word. Enough to acknowledge but not welcome another human being. There was no warmth in it.

"Can I sit down?"

"If you want." She dug her chin into her arm again and swung her feet back and forth together.

Malachi sat cross-legged on the floor next to her and leaned back against the same railings through which Tila spied on the bustling crowds below.

"So...," he said.

"So?"

"So, Ellie told me what happened between you and my dad yesterday," said Malachi.

Tila dropped her gaze to the marketplace, not really focusing on any particular detail.

"You know it bothers her when you don't get along with him."

Tila mumbled something inaudible.

"Huh?"

"I said, what's that got to do with her? It's not like he's her father."

"Wait, are you mad at Ellie, or at my dad?"

"Isn't everyone mad at me?"

Malachi shuffled around to face the same direction as Tila and dropped his legs over the side of the gantry too.

"No, but you don't make it easy sometimes. Look, you know what Ellie's like. She wants everyone to always get along. It's hard for her when people don't."

"By people you mean me."

"She cares about you. Even my dad cares about you really."

"But?"

Malachi sighed. "But he has to care about everyone else as well, and-"

"And I don't?" she challenged, looking at him for the first time.

"No one's saying that. Well, some people are, but he's not. It's just, you know, he has to look at the big picture and manage all the little details at the same time, and you don't."

"But it's not like I don't care."

"I know. I think he knows that too, but you don't... I don't know, you don't blend in."

"You mean I'm not welcome?"

"No, no, no. Not at all! Wait, that sounds wrong. I mean you *are* welcome but you never seem to, uh, commit to the people here. You drop in and out when it suits you."

"Well, why should I commit?" She gestured angrily, taking in the whole market. "This isn't my home. I don't have anything keeping me here. But I still do my part. I work hard and I help people."

Malachi nodded. "That's true, but you're more like a hired hand than a resident."

"I don't take advantage of anyone. I work hard and fair."

"I mean you act more like a visitor than one of the family. That's all I'm saying."

Tila fell silent. She knew this was the crux of it. Eventually she said, "But I'm not one of the family, am I?"

"Neither is Ellie," Malachi pointed out. "She doesn't have anyone else either but she's part of the family. She's a part of the community. She joins in."

"Everyone only loves her because she's cute and harmless."

"No, they love her because she cares, and she gets involved. Without those things she would just be..." Malachi searched for a word.

Tila looked at him for the first time and managed to suppress the involuntary smirk that threatened to break her dark mood. Ellie could do that, even when she wasn't around. "Annoying?" she offered.

Malachi laughed. "Maybe. That's one word for it."

Tila worried her chin against her wrist again and felt the small bones in her wrist shift under the pressure. "Well, she is annoying sometimes."

Malachi smiled to himself. She wasn't wrong. "But you love her anyway, right?"

Tila threw back her head in defeat. "Fine! Yes. I love her even though she can be annoying." She threw him a look. "Just like you!" She curled her legs up on the floor beside her and climbed to her feet. She offered Malachi a hand and helped him up. "I'm sorry," she said, squeezing his hand.

Malachi squeezed Tila's in return. "That's all I wanted to hear. Now let's go and buy stuff." "Good one. With what?"

"Let's go and pretend we can buy stuff."

The market occupied an old tiered arena, so it was wider at the top than at the bottom. It was like being on the inside of an inverted pyramid.

The lowest part, which attracted the most people and the most popular traders, was also the shortest way to travel from one side to the other.

On this occasion the shortest way was not the fastest way. The market was packed, and Malachi and Tila found it impossible to move from stall to stall without shouldering their way through the throngs of buyers and sellers.

"How come it's so crazy in here today?" Tila said.

"You didn't hear? Some trading vessel had engine trouble while transiting the system. Luckily there was someone here with the skills to repair it."

"Let me guess. Your dad?"

"And the best part is that everything they had on board was still fresh. It would have spoiled by the time they reached their destination so he made a deal with them to accept the food as part payment."

"Looks like everyone else heard about it too. Anyway, you didn't hear about it, your dad just told you."

"I guess so."

"So why didn't you just say so? You're always so coy about what you know, Mal. If you know something, say it. You should be more direct."

"Because that always works out so well for you?" Malachi teased.

"Shut up," she said affectionately.

"So, anyway, they get cheap repairs and we get a shipment of fresh food."

"Just one of the many benefits of Juggernaut life." Tila said sarcastically.

"We sure do have it good."

They waded through the crowds until they found shelter in the lee of a stall selling used clothing shipped in from Commonwealth planets.

"Do you know where they're docked?" Tila asked as she unconsciously brushed the back of her hand along a scarf of synthetic silk.

"Bay one. It's the biggest bay this close to the market."

"Ugh. That's near where they sell all the junk."

"Junk?"

"Yeah, scraps of cable, engine parts, whatever fascinating equipment they have that can fix the AG units."

"I heard you, and I said 'Junk?' Anyway, artificial gravity units are quite important out here. You know, what with all the space and all."

"Yeah, but it's not like you can eat them."

"Finding new and exciting food is not the most important thing."

She dropped the scarf and held up a finger to make sure Malachi listed her to her point. "Yes, it is!" she corrected him. "It is the most important thing, especially around here. Think about it. We might get all the potatoes and processed algae we can dream of but basically, we only get what no other planet wants.

"You forgot mushrooms."

"Ugh, mushrooms. Look, the only real meat we get is from the rat farms. Imagine what Commonwealth planets get to eat! When was the last time you ate fruit that was even close to fresh? I mean, how is it we can travel between stars but still can't preserve a strawberry?"

"I know, I know. Our priorities are all wrong!"

"Strawberries are not even that big."

"I don't think size is the problem they are trying to solve, Tila."

"It's still important," she said.

The crowd thinned and they struck out again.

"I remember grapes," Malachi said wistfully. "They were so, sweet, and juicy..."

"And they would burst in your mouth like a...like a...flavour popping."

They sighed together over sweet childhood memories until a voice intruded.

"You two are always talking about the things you remember from planets. When are you going to show me?!"

"Ellie!" said Tila.

Ellie folded her arms and waited for Tila to continue. She tried to look angry, but the effect was spoiled by the flow of people constantly bumping into her which made her lose her balance and then apologize for being in the way.

"Aren't you going to say sorry?" Ellie finally demanded when she could steady herself once more.

"Oh, the party. I'm sorry Ellie, but he just...you know, gets to me."

Ellie pointed at Malachi. "Not to me, to him. It was his father's party you ruined."

Tila stiffened. "Ruined?"

Malachi quickly stepped in to defuse the situation before it could escalate any further. He might have already had Tila's apology, but he knew she took a while to cool down properly.

"It's ok, Ellie. We've talked about it. She's apologised."

Ellie glare at Tila some more until Tila was kind enough to attempt a contrite expression. Then the cloud passed from Ellie's face and they were friends again.

"Well, good. I'm glad that's settled. Are you looking for the food delivery? It's this way." She turned and led them on to Docking Bay One.

"What was that all about?" Tila whispered to Malachi when Ellie was out of earshot.

"She's just looking out for me. She would do that same for you."

"I know, but it's strange watching her be angry. It's like being threatened by a kitten."

When they reached the docking bay the crowds were too deep for them to pass. This rare opportunity was not to be missed. Tila could feel the anticipation in the recycled air.

Someone had taken charge of the crowd and organised them into a line. One person was being let into the docking bay for each one who departed.

Those waiting for their turn were a jumble of curious residents and professional traders, each jockeying for position, each looking to buy or barter as much fresh food as they could carry or afford.

The residents wanted to eat it there and then, but the traders were just as eager to resell their merchandise at a profit margin which would fall somewhere between healthy and outrageous.

The cargo transport *Orion* barely fit in the bay. It squatted before the great docking bay doors which led to the space dock entrance. The ship's name was stencilled in huge white letters above the open cargo ramp and over the primary port and starboard engine housings.

Crew members were shifting items down the cargo ramp and onto the deck where they were being sold and claimed as fast as they could be removed from the ship.

Tila grumbled, "We can't buy anything anyway. Why do we have to wait in line?" It seemed the slow minutes of steady shuffling had brought them no closer to the front of the line. It wasn't just the wait that was getting on her nerves. Malachi's enthusiasm was starting to grate.

"Because I want to see this ship for myself," he said. "My dad said I should look at the ship now in case he decides to punish me by not letting me help him fix it."

"That's a punishment?" said Ellie.

"Punish you for what?" said Tila.

"Your birthday present," said Malachi without turning around.

"Oh."

"If it's so amazing why did it break down?" Ellie asked.

Malachi shrugged. "He doesn't know. Maybe they just hadn't bedded in the design yet. Could be anything."

"How come older ships don't break down here," said Ellie.

"Ellie, the older ships don't even come here because their crews know how dangerous this system is," said Tila.

"If only that were true. You know most ships would avoid this system if they could, but until they can build new beacons for longer range jumps Celato is still the fastest route for most trade.

A thought occurred to Ellie. "Why is Theo punishing you? Tila's the one who went to the Eclipse."

"I'm the one who told her where it was. I was supposed to stop her from going, not help her find it."

"Didn't you tell him you couldn't stop me even if you wanted to?" said Tila.

"No. Believe it or not I didn't tell him that!"

"It might have helped," she offered.

"It might!"

Eventually their long slow shuffle brought them to the threshold of the docking bay. The shouts of the traders haggling with the crew and arguing with each other were magnified by the cavernous space as echoes reverberated around the chamber.

Once through the bay doors Malachi started impatiently hopping in and out of the queue trying to see more of the ship's design. He was the only person there looking up. Everyone else was intent on buying anything and everything they could before someone else beat them to it.

"Back in line," warned one of the crew, wary that anyone from the Juggernaut would be taking an interest in his valuable ship. None of the crew wanted to be here, and they had no intention of making the best of this bad situation. They wanted out of here now. As far as they were concerned they needed to make what money they could before their stock was worthless and get their ship repaired and underway as soon as possible.

Besides, everyone knew you couldn't trust the dispossessed. *Orion's* crew knew full well that if you were stuck here it was because you deserved it. Of course, had they made this opinion public someone might well have pointed out to them that they too were stuck here, and might remain so if it weren't for the help of the people they scorned.

But this was still the popular view shared by most of the Commonwealth, right up to the point where they had nowhere else to go.

Disappointed, Malachi took his place back in the queue and the shuffling continued. By the time they reached the front the ship's crew had decided that rather than selling to the traders, they could sell direct, increase the prices and keep the difference. The upside was a wider range of produce. The downside was the price.

"How much for an orange?" Tila asked a crewman when her turn finally came.

He told her.

"What?!" said Tila.

"Come on!" said Malachi.

"Is that a lot?" said Ellie.

They looked at her.

"I don't know! I've never had one!" she explained.

"We still have enough for one," said Malachi.

"It's the last one," said the crewman. "You want it or not?"

"Fine!" said Tila. "We'll take it."

Malachi paid, Tila grumbled and Ellie bit her lip in anticipation as they moved to one side of the crowd and left the docking bay.

Behind them the crewman tossed the empty container aside and pulled out another box full of oranges.

"Dirt-dwellers think they can do what they like!" said Malachi.

"You were a dirt-dweller once," Ellie said.

"But I never overcharged for an orange. One orange!" He continued grumbling as they returned to the market.

They paused between two stalls. Tila cradled the fruit in her hands, rediscovering the smooth rippled texture of the skin. She offered it to Ellie.

"Have you ever smelled an orange? Try it. Scratch the skin. It's ok, it's tough, you won't damage the inside."

Ellie's face lit up. "Oh, wow!"

"It's even better inside," Tila promised. She cut into the skin by running her thumbnail across the surface and savoured the fine citrus spray she released. Then, taking care not to damage the soft white-veined flesh of the fruit, Tila peeled back the skin and extracted the segments inside.

"Are you ready?" asked Tila as she shared out the pieces, "It's been years since I had one of these."

"On three?" said Malachi. Tila held up three fingers to start a countdown. On one they each took a bite and shared a happy sigh.

Tila sat down in their little alcove and leaned against one of the stalls as she savoured her treat.

The stalls either side of them were almost buried beneath piles of scrap metal, pipework and cables. It looked like someone had torn apart some huge machine and left the pieces where they fell.

Malachi poked around for anything he thought might be useful while Ellie settled herself beside Tila.

Ellie ate her portion delicately, one piece at a time.

Tila wolfed hers down, then checked the stallholder was looking the other way. "Is he looking for new tech?" she asked Ellie as she surreptitiously wiped her fingers on the cloth draped over the table.

"You mean old tech," said Ellie.

"What's new in this place?" said Malachi. He had finished his orange too and was using both hands to look for buried treasure. He seemed fascinated by everything on offer but as far as Ellie and Tila were concerned it was still only junk.

Ellie delicately sucked orange juice from her fingertips. She hated getting her hands sticky. "I don't know what you expect to find," she said to Malachi, "Nothing that old is going to work anyway."

"What if I told you that I was looking for something for your racer?"

"Oh, then please carry on!"

"Anyway, Tila's staff is old and works fine," Malachi replied without looking up. "It's paleotech for sure."

"So you keep saying, but we don't *know* if it's paleotech," said Tila, dismissing his opinion with a wave of her hand. "We don't even know what it's made of."

"All the more reason," Malachi said as if this were obvious. "You have to admit, it checks all the right boxes." He counted off fingers. "One, we don't know where it comes from. Two, we don't know what it's made of and three, we don't know what it's for or how it works. Uh, four. So it must predate the war."

"So how do you know it works properly if you don't know what it does?" said Ellie.

"I know how it works, and I know it's a weapon. And I know without it I wouldn't be here now." Tila said. "I don't need to know any more than that."

"Maybe you should find out what it's worth," urged Ellie, "Then we can buy our way out of here."

"I'm not selling it. Ever. We've come a long way together. It's worth too much to me."

"But how much is it worth to *me*?" Ellie said with a grin.

There was a cough behind them. "Excuse me, ladies, did one of you mention paleotech?" His eyes darted to the short staff on Tila's back, evidence enough he had overheard their conversation.

"It's not for sale," Tila said quickly.

"Oh, I understand! Really, I do. But items like this don't pass through here every day. Could I at least look at it? Maybe I can tell you what it's worth?"

"It's not for sale, there's no point. I don't care what it's worth," repeated Tila.

"You don't care what it's worth?" He sounded appalled at the idea. "But it could be ancient tech, before we lost contact with Earth. It could even be *from* Earth! How can you not want to know?"

"Because none of that matters to me. I don't care where it came from, or how old it might be. It's mine now."

"But..."

"It's not for sale, and no, you can't touch it." Tila said firmly to stop him leading the conversation where she knew it was going. "And stop romanticising everything, you too Malachi. It was barely a hundred years ago we lost contact with Earth. It's hardly ancient technology."

He grumbled something, realised there was no profit to be made here and vanished behind his stall, muttering to himself. A few seconds later he reappeared with a broom. This time he was brusque and demanding. "You can't sit there."

The girls looked up into a scowl that resembled a face.

"You can't sit there. You have to move," he repeated.

"We're not in the way," protested Ellie.

"You can't sit there. This is my space for my trade. Clear off. You want to sit there you can rent the space."

Ellie tried again, "We weren't in the way a moment ago. We're not stopping anyone. Tila?"

"Come on, Ellie. Not today. I'm trying to be *less* confrontational, remember?"

They gathered their things. Malachi reluctantly tore himself away from the parts on offer. Tila held her staff close to her body to ward off curious hands. Ellie continued to grumble, and together they dived back into the fast-flowing waters of the market.

6

They wandered through the market awhile longer. Malachi led the way, idly browsing things they didn't need and couldn't afford. Then Tila suddenly realised where they were headed.

She nudged Ellie and pointed at Malachi. A look of puzzlement crossed Ellie's face, then she understood what Tila was trying to tell her. She grinned at Tila, held her gaze and asked innocently, "Hey, Malachi. Where are we going?"

"Uh, nowhere. Why?"

"Nowhere?" said Tila.

"Oh," said Ellie, "because I thought we were heading toward Nina's stall."

Malachi had his back to them but the girls knew he was blushing.

"Well, as we're in the area I just thought..." he trailed off into an unintelligible mumble. No plausible excuses came to mind.

"Thought what?" said Tila, who had no intention of letting Malachi off the hook too easily.

"I thought she might have something new for me," he finished helplessly.

"Something new like...?"

"Like news on ships," Malachi said, now more confident in his lie. "I don't know how she keeps up with it but she's always one step ahead of everyone else."

"So, that must be why she's so popular," said Tila. "It's good of her to let him know, isn't it, Ellie?"

"Why yes, Tila, it is!" Ellie's voice dripped with good-natured sarcasm.

"They must be getting on very well!"

"Yes, very well!"

"Shut up," said Malachi, refusing to turn around and see their grinning faces. "Anyway, my dad asks me to see her sometimes. She's a good information broker."

"I bet she is," said Tila. "Did he ask you today?" Ellie had to bite her tongue to keep from laughing.

"Shut up," he repeated.

The turned away from the central market area and headed for one of the terraces, where services and information rather than products and goods, were always on offer. Many of the services available would be illegal on any other space station but on the Juggernaut there was no law.

Malachi ignored the giggling and whispers behind him.

"Hey, Mal," said Tila, "How does Nina always know when new ships are coming in, anyway? There must be hundreds of people all over the Juggernaut wanting the same thing."

Grateful for a sensible question at last, Malachi said, "She pays people to look out for her, for one thing, and don't forget how big this place is. New ships arrive almost every week but no one can keep watch over the whole city. She makes sure she's the first to know about any new salvage. Otherwise someone else will strip them first. Plus, I gave her a list of parts we need in the shop so if anything comes in she sends me a message."

"What if someone else wants the same parts?" said Ellie.

"I don't know. It's never been a problem."

Ellie and Tila exchanged a wink.

"Why is that, do you think?" Tila asked innocently.

"I don't know. Why?"

"Oh, nothing," said Tila.

By now they had climbed a third of the way up the terraces. From here they had a commanding view of the main trading area below them. Tiers of stalls spanned out to either side, encircling the room, and more than a dozen more rose to the ceiling above them. Each level up had fewer stalls than the tier below until the top three levels were almost empty.

Malachi led them to an empty table only one turning from the main staircase. Screens had been erected behind the table. Each one scrolled slowly through pages and pages of indecipherable technical data.

Malachi rapped on the table. "Hey, Quinn? You around?"

A woman, young, but still several years older than Malachi, stepped into view from behind the screens. Dark red hair spilled down one shoulder over skin the colour of almonds and crowned an assortment of pen-sized tools clipped to her white coveralls.

She held a data tablet in one hand and a stylus in the other. Her wide-eyed broad smile faltered when she realised that Malachi was not alone.

"I thought I recognised your voice." She flicked her hair back over her shoulder with an effortless cool that Ellie envied and Tila was sure she practised. "Hi, Malachi."

Ellie and Tila exchanged a silent high-five behind his back.

"Hi, Nina."

They stared at each other for a moment, saying nothing. When the silence became uncomfortable Ellie poked Malachi in the back. He jumped and started up again like a broken toy that needed a push.

"Oh, uh, did you have anything new for me?"

Ellie looked at Tila again and rolled her eyes. "Terrible!" she whispered to Tila. Tila pulled Ellie away from the table and they made a show of pretending to study one of the technical displays.

"Give him a chance," Tila whispered back.

Together they faced the screen but paid it no attention. Instead they watched Nina and Malachi in the reflection and on listened to Malachi's attempt at small-talk.

It was painful.

"He should say something about her hair," Ellie whispered.

"Or anything that doesn't involve a machine," Tila agreed.

After overhearing a few more awkward exchanges Ellie decided she couldn't take any more and turned around. "Malachi!" she snapped, "Didn't you say you were coming here to see what Nina had to give you?"

"Oh. Uh, yeah I think-" Malachi began.

"I have your list here somewhere..." said Nina.

Ellie rolled her eyes as she watched them fumble through around the stall looking for the inventory.

"Why are you rushing them?" Tila whispered.

"I was trying to get them to hurry up and decide if they like each other. I didn't mean for them to start talking business."

"You broke the spell. You pushed them too quick and too hard and made them uncomfortable."

Ellie was impressed at Tila's observation from her friend. Perhaps there was hope for her, too.

"That's very insightful, Tila."

Tila shrugged. "I have layers."

"So, since when did you become an expert on flirting?"

"I haven't always lived here, you know," she winked. "Anyway, when did you? I've never seen you flirt."

"I'm not that sort of girl, Tila."

Nina finally found what she was looking for and handed Malachi a datapad showing her long and detailed inventory. "Do you know how to use this model?" she asked him hope-fully.

"Say no," Ellie whispered into the screen.

"I got it, thanks." Malachi input some com-mands and the list was replaced by something considerably shorter.

"Oh, for goodness sake," Ellie said.

"Is this all the recent arrivals?" said Malachi.

"Everything in the last two weeks in these areas." Nina handed him a second datapad which displayed a three-dimensional map of the city. Several locations glowed white. "It's been unusually busy in the last few days. We've had eleven new – well, old – arrivals aban-doned in the system. Four have been fully in-tegrated already. The other seven are still looking for their final resting place."

Malachi nodded. New ships were the funda-mental resource of the Juggernaut. Sometimes they would be stripped for parts or recycled. There was an endless need for repairs and re-placement tech. At other times, they would provide much needed living space.

"Anything interesting nearby?"

Nina touched two of the glowing points nearest to New Haven. "I have people running salvage on the closest ships, here and here, but even they are half a day's journey." She leaned over the data pad to press a button for him. Red hair trailed across the display.

"These are the ship names and everything I know about them."

Malachi traced down the list with his finger as he read the names and possible salvage. "*Blue September* is a private shuttle. I doubt we will find anything there we don't already have in the workshop. The *Lesnar* looks promising if we can get there in time. *Far Horizon* could be useful. Haulers like that have good power-to-weight ratio's and-"

"What did you say?" said Tila sharply.

"I said haulers have a good power-to-weight ratio."

"Before that! What was it called?"

"*Far Horizon.*"

"*Far Horizon*? Let me see that!" She pushed between Nina and Malachi and snatched the datapad. "Where is this? Where did it come from?"

"What's the matter? Oh..." said Malachi as realisation dawned.

"What is it?" asked Ellie. She looked at Nina who just shrugged helplessly.

"The *Far Horizon*? Here? How?" Tila said again. She shook the computer at Nina demanding answers.

"Whoa, whoa, calm down. Let me look at it again," said Malachi.

Tila pressed the datapad hard against Malachi's chest, "Tell me."

"Ok, ok, give me a moment." Malachi interrogated the machine further, extracting as much detail as he could.

"You know that ship?" Nina asked Tila as Malachi worked.

Ellie caught up at last. "Oh! The colony mission!" Tila nodded, her face set as she watched Malachi.

"It's not a colony ship," said Nina, puzzled, "it's far too small. Anyway, no one has built one of those for over a decade, not since the last mission blew up because of negligence."

Tila froze Nina with her glare.

"Because of what?" she asked coldly.

"That's just what I heard," she said, "Why, what did you hear?"

Tila glared at Nina. *Will people always think that the failure was my parent's fault?*

"I *heard* that my mother was the captain of the mission, and my father was on board the *Far Horizon* when it vanished."

Nina clamped one hand to her mouth. "Oh, Tila, I'm sorry. I didn't know."

"But you knew they were *negligent*, didn't you? You knew it was their fault. You knew enough about *that*."

Ellie tried to defuse the situation. "Tila," she said softly as she touched her friend's elbow.

"Get off me." Tila shrugged Ellie aside and stepped away from the group.

"Why didn't you tell me?" Nina hissed at Malachi.

Malachi shrugged. "It never came up. Why would it? It was years ago, and she never talks about it anyway," he whispered back. Then, trying to defuse the situation further, he walked over to Tila and said, "It's just a cargo hauler. See?" He passed her the datapad.

Tila studied the small display, not understanding. "But how can it have the same name?" she pleaded.

"There's a lot of ships out there, Tila. Some of them have the same name. Ships only have to have a unique name when registered with the same port authority."

"And every planet is a port authority, and some space-stations, so there could easily be more than one *Far Horizon*," added Nina.

"But...it's the same name." Tila protested again.

Ellie rubbed Tila's arm. She had never seen her friend seem so deflated, so lost.

122

"I think it's just a coincidence, Tila," she said gently.

"I want to see it." Tila said.

"Do you think you should?" Ellie asked carefully, "It might just upset you more."

"I *need* to see it," she demanded again, "I just need to, to...to know."

"Could we?" Malachi asked Nina.

"If you think that will help, sure. I already have someone else due to run salvage on it but I can send them to the *Lesnar* instead. But you'll have to move fast before word spreads and someone else scalps all the best parts." Nina passed Malachi a list of components and closed his hand around it. "Be careful," she told him.

"You really want to go?" Malachi asked Tila.

"Yes."

"And you know that it is half a day from here?" He checked the data again. "More than half a day."

"Please, Malachi," she said. She was almost begging. "I have to. I need to see that ship."

7

The Juggernaut grew like a tumour. In fact, a tumour was the best metaphor anyone had come up with to describe the Juggernaut. It grew slowly, without thought or design, and was big, ugly, dangerous and unwanted.

The original kernel at the heart of the city had long ago been lost to tons of metal which had accumulated around it.

Like an oyster layering nacre around an alien particle, the Juggernaut too had grown, skin by skin, blister by blister, into the titanic beast it had now become. It shared the same process without producing the same beauty.

The Juggernaut attracted wrecks and husks of old ships like refuse did to flies. As more and more people from nearby systems found

themselves among the low ranks of the dispossessed the demand for living space grew rapidly.

The increasing population brought with it a
commensurate increase in the need for power,
light, food, raw materials and the hundred
other things on which a city feeds.

But the city never stopped feeding. Never
stopped growing. Its impossible hunger could
never be sated. The only option was to add
more ships.

In time this mantra became 'add more anything', and residents soon welcomed a diverse
array of hulls and structures which quickly became part of the city.

This growth happened slowly, and, without
any central government or oversight, it took
place haphazardly.

In the long years since the first two ships
were fused together the city had grown in
bumps and bulges, fits and starts.

The fastest growth occurred near docks and
ports as new parts were layered around the
most convenient places for ships to land. In
time these areas became entirely rimmed with
habitation and the ports began to resemble
metal craters on an artificial moon.

The next logical step was to enclose these
craters entirely. Once sealed and pressurised,

they became bubbles of life and beacons of hope. Beacons which attracted the hopeless.

Eventually, inevitably, the new growth would cover the old, further burying the past in the artificial stratum of cable and steel.

And so the city grew.

Some unconscious instinct of design had meant the city had grown longer than wider, and wider than taller.

From a distance the Juggernaut appeared like a giant flattened and misshapen potato, aligned along its vector.

But despite the hope and home it offered to hundreds of thousands there could be no happy ending in store for the city. It lived in a decaying orbit and tumbled slowly through space with nothing able to stop its growth, or its eventual impact with the sun.

No one could stop it, so they called it the Juggernaut.

In space there is no up or down, and yet human ingenuity, boundless and resourceful, had found a point of reference. The orbital plane of the star had become the compass by which starships sailed. The solar north became up, and the solar south became down.

But the Juggernaut was no space station. It had no planned orbit. It spiralled through space, so there was no common up or down on which to agree.

This meant that it was not uncommon for travellers on foot to have to adjust themselves to the local gravity field.

So, it was a wise and wary traveller who paid close attention to the clues before them. Dirt and debris gathered unnaturally in a corner, or corridors lit from the side, rather than from above, would all be signposts that the conditions ahead may not be as expected. The next airlock could see the floor become a wall with one step.

Tila had spent days and weeks exploring the regions around New Haven and had trained herself to become alert to all the subtle changes in the environment. She was a wise and wary traveller.

Malachi spent most of his time in the workshop elbow-deep inside an engine. A wise and wary traveller he was not.

"Humph," he said as he fell sideways against a wall which had rudely and suddenly become a floor. From his point of view Tila and Ellie appeared to be standing on the wall.

He had stepped into a gravity shelf set at ninety degrees from the previous room. His down had become his left in the space of one footstep and gravity had grabbed him and pulled him sideways at an irresistible nine-point-eight metres per second. Then it had dumped him, ungraciously, on the new floor.

The girls supported each other as they manoeuvred more carefully into the new gravity zone. Tila made it look effortless as she seemed to roll from one section to another without missing a beat.

"You could have told me," he accused, rubbing his elbow where it had knocked against the wall. *Floor*, he reminded himself.

"That's right, I could have," Tila agreed, "But Ellie asked me not to."

Ellie's jaw dropped.

"I did not!" she said to Tila. "I didn't," she repeated, this time for Malachi's benefit.

"What did you say then?" Tila challenged.

"I said *what if* you don't tell him?"

"See?" said Tila.

Malachi brushed himself off and climbed to his feet.

"Har-har," said Malachi, not laughing.

"Where to now? This passageway splits up ahead," Tila asked.

"I'd check the map but I think my arm is broken," Malachi complained.

Tila clapped him on both shoulders. "You seem fine to me. Are you sure you can go on?"

"I'll manage."

He pulled his map free and worked out their location. Despite Tila's joke he knew she was still concerned. She wouldn't be making this journey, this deep, without a good reason.

Malachi thought she was overly worried about finding the ship. He didn't think it would amount to anything. Ship names were reused all the time under different ports and registration authorities. So what if there was another ship named *Far Horizon*? It didn't mean anything.

What had happened to her all those years ago was tragic, he wasn't denying that, but he hoped she would have the sense to realise that this was going to be a fruitless chase. He knew grief could be a powerful motivator, but he had always thought of Tila as the strong one of their trio.

The map showed they were still on the right path. Their destination wasn't far. The only thing still nagging at him was that their path had led them so deep inside the Juggernaut, far deeper than he would have expected for a ship that had only arrived in recent weeks. Not only that, but if it was from the *Far Horizon* that would only make it about twelve years old, and who would abandon a ship here that had barely a decade of use?

So it must be a different ship, an older ship, he told himself. It was the only thing that made sense.

"This way." He pointed toward the left passage at last. "It's this way."

8

Ellie tensed, jumped and grabbed hold of the lip of the access hatch. Malachi reached down from the shadows above and gave Ellie his hand. Ellie took it, Malachi pulled her up and Ellie wriggled through the opening. Once through the hatch she sat on the dirty floor and dangled her legs through the hole.

Tila flashed a light around the cramped space while Malachi scattered glowcubes around the cabin.

"Is this the right place?" Ellie asked before climbing to her feet. "I didn't see a name outside."

"This is it," said Malachi. "Well, the right location anyway. Looks like the name got scratched away when they shoved it in here. There'll be a nameplate somewhere in here, anyway."

Tila scanned the room by flashlight while the cubes slowly came to life.

Malachi pulled two more flashlights from his pocket. He gave one to Ellie and clicked on the other.

"Do you carry spares of everything?" said Tila.

"You can't be too prepared," he replied as he ducked underneath a console to inspect it.

"It's a bit small for a cargo ship," said Ellie, calculating the ship's volume from what she could see.

"It was a hauler, not a transport," said Malachi. His voice came back muffled beneath the console. "This is just the rear cabin. A hauler is basically a tug which pulls a shipping spine full of cargo pods. They stick thrusters on the other end to make it go. That hatch we came through would connect to a habitation module for longer journeys."

Ellie smiled to herself in the dark. It amused her that Malachi was always ready to teach. "I love that you know everything," she said.

"Some things," said Malachi.

Tila leaned over a console and wiped the sticky dirt from the display with her fingertips. The cabin wall above the desk crumpled inward, as if the hauler had been forced into a hole that was too small.

"He doesn't know everything," she said, "Ask him how to cook."

"Hey!" Malachi protested, "I can cook."

"You can't," said Tila, without looking up.

"She's right though," said Ellie. "You cooked for me once."

"Just once?" said Malachi. He tried to remember when that happened.

"Mmm hmm. I never let you do it again."

Tila smiled into her shoulder and pressed switches at random. Maybe there was still some life in the batteries. They were real switches, not smooth glass touch panels. Nothing worked. She straightened up. "So, all we have is a cockpit?" she asked.

"This is just the rear cabin. The main cockpit is through there," Malachi replied, and pointed at a door Tila had assumed was a closet.

Ellie touched a finger to the door control mounted in the frame. "There's no power."

"Can we force it open?" said Tila.

"Try the manual release," suggested Malachi, pointing to a spot over her head.

Tila reached up and unclipped a panel covered with faded instructions. Inside was a red handle. She yanked it sharply and something *clunked* inside the recessed mechanism. The cabin door opened an inch.

She tugged at the lip of the door with her fingertips but could barely move it any further.

"Can you help me?" she asked Malachi.

Malachi edged his way past Ellie, squeezed one hand into the gap, took hold of a grab handle with his other hand and pulled hard. The door shot open with a loud crack. More dust billowed up from door frame which made them cough.

The cabin was a standard commercial design. It was practical, efficient, and entirely lacking in imagination.

Two chairs, once white and new but now covered in the same fine dark powder as everything else, sat before a cracked command console which filled the width of the cabin. The three-paned view-port had smashed open when the ship had been wedged into its final home.

The impact had crushed and twisted the nose of the hauler. Evidently, an air-tight seal still existed somewhere or the cabin would have de-pressurised and they would all be breathing vacuum by now. Even deep inside the city people had to be alert to leaks.

What remained was damp and surprisingly cold, most likely the result of an old coolant leak nearby.

The madescent air chilled them through their clothes and made dusty surfaces become grime to the touch.

The moist atmosphere had corroded any wiring exposed by the impact. Broken electronics hung from the underside of the console. A myriad of electronic and mechanical crumbs littered the dirty floor.

Malachi dropped into the pilot seat and blew hard at the dirt covering the controls. Only a few particles danced free from the damp film which trapped them on the glass and metal surfaces.

Tila surveyed the scene with doubt. "Nina was right, someone did get here before us after all."

"They can't have," said Malachi. "The hatch was sealed. We must be first."

"So why is it such a wreck?" asked Ellie as she poked her head into the room. Her breath misted faintly in the chill air.

"I don't know, but not all of this damage was accidental." He waved a hand over the console. "Maybe the screens, but not this."

Tila slumped into the co-pilot seat. She didn't know what she had expected to find here. Part of her fantasised about opening the door and finding all the answers she wanted neatly wrapped up and awaiting her arrival, but life was rarely so accommodating. Even so, she had hoped for more than a battered old cabin that had been squeezed into the pock-ravaged skin of the Juggernaut.

It's not like anyone could even have piloted the ship in here, she thought. The ship had simply been forced into a hole to be forgotten.

Ellie and Malachi were by this time deep in the underside of the main flight console. Tila could tell what they were doing from the noises. She heard Malachi pushing through a mass of dangling wires, then call for Ellie's flashlight. They swapped places. Malachi passed Ellie a tool and directed her smaller hands in some task his own hands were too big for.

She heard wires being snipped. Then a component of some kind, unrecognisable to Tila, appeared on the floor next to her.

"Keep this," said Malachi.

She picked it up and placed it on the empty seat beside her. She heard another snip, then a tearing sound as Malachi or Ellie ripped something free from the console. This appeared on the floor too.

"Junk," said Malachi.

Tila placed this on the chair, too. Over the next few minutes more things appeared. Malachi said 'keep it', or 'junk it', and Tila placed it in the correct pile. Malachi was obviously taking care with the items he wanted to keep. That pile of components had been neatly trimmed away from their housings. The items he didn't want had simply been ripped out to make room.

Tila stared blankly at the heap of discarded electronics. Frayed wires sprouted from each item like a rooting seed. Like her, they were useless now. Malachi and Ellie were doing the work. She just had to sit here and wait. She half-smiled to herself. *Hopefully I have more to offer than a frayed wire,* she thought.

She dragged a fingertip over the filthy console without realising she was tracing out letters.

"How did this place get so dirty, anyway? It hasn't been here long, and it doesn't look that old," she asked.

Malachi's hand appeared from underneath the console and his fingers wiped through the dirt. The hand vanished again. Malachi sniffed it the dirt and rubbed the residue between finger and thumb. "It looks mineral to me. Maybe this was hauling rocks or soil? It gets everywhere if the crew are sloppy. All these surfaces should be sealed during normal operations." He threw an old rag at her leg. "Here, use this, and see what else you can find in there."

Tila wiped the worst of the dirt from her fingers as Malachi returned to his work. In truth, there wasn't much to see. The row of small lockers at the back were empty. Any items in there had been removed long ago.

The first-aid kit was gone, which was a shame. Medical supplies of any kind were always in demand. Even the fire extinguishers had been removed from their bright orange plinths. The high visibility signs above them pointed to nothing.

Tila used the rag to wipe the console clean for something to do, grateful that some things were as simple as they appeared. The dirt gave way to reveal the perfectly smooth glass surface beneath. Almost perfectly smooth. Her actions revealed a shallow, oval indentation at the top of the console. At each side was an empty screw hole. *They even took the name badge.*

"Ow!" Malachi's exclamation jolted Tila from her thoughts.

Ellie pulled her head out of the console desk. "You ok?" she asked.

"It's nothing, just a sharp edge."

"Let me look," said Tila.

Malachi rolled his eyes at her concern. "It's nothing. Really. Look, see? Just a little cut." He presented his wound with a flourish.

138

He was right, it was just a minor cut. Mollified, Tila sat back in her chair. *Just a little cut.* The thought gnawed at her brain. She mentally shook her head to clear her mind.

"What are you going to do with those?" She pointed at the pile of broken electronics with her toe.

"That's what I asked him," said Ellie. She stood and stretched to work out the kinks that had developed in the cramped workspace.

"No, you asked what was I going to do with all this junk," accused Malachi.

"Same difference."

The familiar sound of good-natured banter between her friends relaxed Tila. "So, what is it for?" she repeated.

"Some are spares, some are just for fun," said Malachi.

"Isn't this too old to be useful?"

"Some of this tech is less than fifteen years old. We're getting by with parts much older than this. We couldn't buy this tech in the city. It's not like anyone cuts their prices for us."

Tila frowned. That word again. It wanted attention. "Be honest with me Mal, do you think this ship came from the colony mission?"

Malachi thought for a moment before answering. The truth wasn't always welcome. "I don't think so, Tila. I'm sorry. I wish I could help but I just can't be sure. The thing is, anyone could register a commercial ship with the same name as one of the colony ships as long as they used a different port authority. The transponder chip would confirm it for sure either way but I haven't found it yet."

"Is that unusual?"

He shrugged. "I guess."

Ellie brushed her hair from her eyes with the back of her hand to avoid touching her face with dirty fingers.

"What does a transponder do?"

"It IDs the ship for navigation and fleet comms," Malachi explained.

"You know, the nameplate from the console is missing too," said Tila.

"But we know what the ship is called," Ellie pointed out.

"The nameplate I took from *Orion* had the port authority on it."

"So?"

"So, the nameplate would link this ship to a specific port. We would know which *Far Horizon* this is," Tila replied.

"Ok, that's unusual," Malachi admitted.

"Not if someone is trying to hide what this ship is, or where it's been," she pointed out.

Malachi thought for a moment before he said, "Maybe." He returned to the underside of the console with Ellie and continued to look thoughtful.

Tila watched them start another argument over how best to reach the remaining innards of the console.

Ellie protested that she couldn't reach anything while Malachi continued to insist that she could. He collected more small cuts and scrapes every time Ellie challenged him to reach something she said was too difficult, and then the moment he agreed with her she plucked them out for him anyway.

It dawned on Tila that Ellie made a fuss just so she could prove to Malachi how indispensable she really was. It was obvious now she saw them working together like this. Ellie couldn't do anything apart from win races and look pretty, so when she had the chance she made a big deal about how essential she was. As Tila listened to them bicker, she also realised that Malachi knew. He was kind enough to indulge her.

After declaring at last that there was nothing else of value in the console, Malachi took his tools back from Ellie and began to carefully pry tiny components free from the circuit boards they had cut out. He neatly trimmed back the wires Ellie had cut.

"Sorry, Tila, all the good stuff is gone. The transponder's not there. We looked, but..." He left the sentence hanging.

"We?" said Ellie, wiping her dirty hands on the upholstered seat-back. Without looking Malachi threw some small, useless part at her which bounced off her forehead.

Tila sighed. This was going nowhere. She wanted answers, but most of all she wanted hope. So far, all she had gained from their expedition was more questions. But somehow the ship *felt* wrong. It nagged at her, this little hauler buried so far inside the city. It should have been at the surface.

But what reason would anyone have to hide it? It was just a hauler. It had no value.

So why did it bother her?

Tila stared at the blade in Malachi's hand.

"Mal."

"Yeah?"

"How come there are so many chips missing?"

"Probably because another salvage team went over the ship before it was abandoned here."

"So they took out anything valuable?"

"Yeah, they got most of it. I'm only taking what they left behind."

She paused to think this through. There was a question she needed to ask but she didn't know what it was. It taunted her from just beneath the surface of her mind. Just out of reach. She asked another instead. "Why are you being so careful with that knife?"

"Because I don't want to damage anything, obviously. Ellie, can you hold that light a little higher for me?"

"So how come everything else has been ripped out? I mean, if it was valuable, wouldn't they have been more careful, like you are being? Why risk the damage?"

Malachi hesitated. He dropped his hands to his lap. "What are you saying?"

"Maybe it wasn't a salvage team, maybe someone was in a hurry and ripped those parts out so we couldn't find them."

Malachi sighed and waved his tool like he was teaching a class. "Tila, I see what you're thinking, but they could have just deleted the data if they wanted."

"But they *didn't*, did they? Deleting it wasn't enough. You're the engineer Mal, why would they do that?"

"You think this ship has been cleaned out so no one knows what it is? That it's from your *Far Horizon*, and someone is trying to hide it?"

"Maybe."

"Come on, really?"

It sounded silly when she heard it from someone else's lips. And yet.

And yet.

Ellie joined in for the first time. "We couldn't find the transponder, and you said that was unusual. And I couldn't find the navigation data chip you wanted either."

"Yeah, but-" Malachi began.

"Hold on," interrupted Tila, "So this ship is hidden away, *and* it's missing any sort of ID and now we don't even know where it's been?"

"But not everything's missing, look at all the chips I did find."

"What are they?"

He pointed them out one by one. "This one controls the fuel mix, this provides baseline calibration for life support, this one talks to the gyroscope-"

"Which one controls navigation? Or comms? Or flight plans?"

"None of these do, but-"

"Malachi, have you found anything, anything at all, that tells us what this ship is, or where it has been?"

He hesitated.

"Mal?"

"You're going to take this the wrong way. I don't want to get your hopes up," said Malachi carefully.

"Because?"

"The comms buffer is missing, but this was a part of it. I think it got caught up in the wires when they pulled the rest of it free." He picked up a small black square the size of her thumbnail and held it out in his palm.

"What is it?"

"I don't know exactly. It's not one of the primary components. It could be a metadata store or a sub-processor."

Tila turned the tiny chip over in her hands, looking for some clue, some piece of information that meant her journey didn't have to end here.

"So, it's probably as useless as every other thing in this stupid shuttle!" She made to throw it back on the floor in frustration but Ellie stopped her and took the chip from Tila's hand.

She held it between finger and thumb and examined it by flashlight. "Metadata? That's like data about data, right?" she said to Malachi.

"That's right, like the address or the timestamp, but not the actual message."

"So, it *is* useless," Tila repeated.

Ellie flapped her hand in Tila's face to shut her up. "Wait!" she ordered. "Does that mean you can find out where and when messages were sent?"

Malachi's jaw dropped. "Ellie, you're a genius!"

"I am? I mean, I am!"

"How does that help?" Tila asked.

"There's nothing in this cabin that links it to the colony expedition but if we can find any evidence of messages sent to or received from the *Far Horizon* after the colony ship vanished-"

"It would mean they survived the Jump," finished Tila.

"Maybe it's not useless after all," said Ellie as she gave it back to Tila.

"Come to the workshop tomorrow. I'll see what I can find out," Malachi said.

Tila closed her fingers around the chip, not crushing it, but forming a tight protective barrier with her fist. She studied her knuckles as she folded her thumb over her fingers.

"I know I saw two ships destroyed and one disappear. In the last twelve years no one has had any answers for me." She stood up and held out the chip. "If this even has a hint of an answer, I want to know what it is."

9

The next day they gathered at Malachi's workshop to see what he had learned from the chip.

The workshop was always a mess, and Tila remembered why she avoided it. Apart from her unsettled relationship with Malachi's father she hated the disarray. She liked things neat and ordered.

Malachi sat at one end of a low hanger on a high stool in front of a workbench covered in diagnostic tools. The space behind him was only large enough to accommodate one small transport or two personal vehicles.

Row upon row of metal racking filled the walls either side of him, apart from the doorway, and every inch of shelving was filled with boxes. Each box contained spare parts, or other basic components. Some boxes contained larger items that were either being assembled or disassembled. It was impossible to tell the difference.

Tila had once peeked inside the boxes once. They were neatly organised. Malachi and Theo could easily find any item they wanted very quickly, but apart from their stores, the rest of the room was a mess.

Cables, wires, pipes, tubing, iso-chips, computer cores, broken AI modules, damaged ventilation systems, hydration units, air-filtration housings, waste recycling processors (they all stayed clear of these) and the like, covered almost every surface.

The third wall was home to stores of lubricants and other exotic, and possibly toxic, liquids.

It was partly this lack of space which meant that Theo had to travel as much as did. There was very little room left to bring the work home.

Tila wondered why, for example, someone would need sixteen, apparently identical, tools to remove worn bolts. Theo had once tried to explain to her the difference between clockwise and counter-clockwise threading. The advantages and disadvantages of quad, hex and octo shafts, and the different electrical properties of each type of metal, and why these details were so very important, but Tila had failed to grasp these inscrutable facts.

She had become bored and confused. Theo had become impatient and frustrated, and together they ended up turning something that should have brought them closer into something which drove them further apart.

Tila preferred Malachi's approach to technology. This involved him looking at something, fixing it, and giving it back. She suspected (rightly) that her bored expression had somehow been interpreted by Theo as disrespect, but that couldn't be further from the truth. She had a great deal of respect for Malachi's father. She just didn't like him very much.

Filling the limited space between all these things was Theo's ship. It squatted in the centre of the workshop, its angular bulk hiding the bay doors on the fourth wall.

The ship was clearly built with utility in mind rather than anything that could be mistaken for comfort.

Although an old design it was still eminently practical. Large gull-wing doors on each side of the craft allowed easy access to tools and equipment.

At one time, Theo had considered replacing the gull-wing mechanism with a sliding door to save space. Malachi had instead cleverly re-designed the doors so they could provide easier access to their gear. Now the open doors saved space instead of consuming it.

Bunks inside the ship enabled a crew of three to work on location for extended periods. It was not a luxurious place to spend time, but it made it possible for Theo to undertake work which would not be practical in his workshop, located as it was some distance inside the hull of the Juggernaut.

The fact that the workshop was difficult to access from the outer hull was one of the reasons his family had settled in this area. What it lacked in space and practicality it made up for in the price.

The ship was named the *Rhino* after an animal from earth's past.

Tila had never seen one but Malachi had described it to her. Apparently, the sensor spike mounted on the front of the cabin resembled the creature in some way.

Tila couldn't picture the animal until Malachi showed her on his datapad. Until then she had imagined it to be some sort of giant grey horse.

Horses she had seen. They, along with hundreds of other examples of plant and animal life from earth, had been carried out into the stars as humanity expanded its heavenly realm.

Tila knew describing animals could be difficult. She had once tried to describe a horse to Ellie. Based on Tila's description Ellie had pictured them as ugly, hairy creatures with big noses. The more Tila tried to correct this image the more caricatured the creature became in Ellie's imagination.

"When you describe it back to me you make it sound like an Elephant," Tila had protested.

"What's a 'Nelliphant'?" Ellie had asked.

"Never mind."

The years of dirt had almost won their battle to hide the *Rhino's* burnt-orange paintwork. It hugged the recessed corners and cracks of the hull. In stark contrast were the fresh, sharp metal scars and specular highlights on the raised edges and corners of the metal. It seemed the evidence of age and wear could make itself known no matter how proud you stood or how deep you hid.

And it was clearly a ship designed for space travel. Even Tila could see that. The hard, angled surfaces gave it all the aerodynamic efficiency of a brick.

The *Rhino* was the single most important item in the workshop, possibly the most important in all New Haven. It brought in trade, materials and supplies, and enabled the residents to travel to other communities by flying direct, rather than taking the dangerous paths through the city.

Most residents didn't count the tiny one-person racers built from spare parts as an acceptably safe option. Without the *Rhino*, and without Theo, New Haven would not have been able to blossom like a flower in the dirt.

The wide main thruster was located high on the body of the craft, and because of this design feature the ship only just fit into the workshop.

Even this was a minor miracle, made possible only because the landing gear had been modified to prevent its full deployment. It meant a steady hand was needed at the controls but it allowed the *Rhino* to fly in and out of the workshop.

Malachi had pointed out to his father that they may as well remove the landing gear altogether, but his father was always one for doing things the right way.

Early in their friendship, Malachi and Tila had concluded that the right way was often Theo's way. But just as often, and especially in matters of planning, and bringing New Haven to life, Theo's way had, time and again, proved to be the right way.

Tila almost wished that Theo was here now. Almost.

She imagined he would pick up the damaged chip they had salvaged from the shuttle, look at it from all angles then rattle off a list of items he would need to solve the problem at hand while Malachi would fetch and carry things from the workshop stores to meet this list of demands.

It annoyed her that Theo would treat Malachi as just another part in a machine.

"I know he says there is a place for everything but he doesn't mean you," she had explained to him, too loudly, one time when she had lost her patience while trying to encourage him to stand up for himself.

"I'm just doing my part, that's all," Malachi had told her.

"It's always your turn," she had told him, "Why can't someone else do all the running around for a change?"

"Because there is no one else! It's my responsibility!" he had shouted back, and that ended the conversation.

Tila sensed that Malachi had avoided her in the days immediately following their fight. She hoped he had been thinking about what she had said, but she suspected he was just angry with her for pushing him to be something he didn't want to be.

But there's nothing wrong with making your own way through life, she thought. *And there's nothing wrong with being independent. He shouldn't have to take orders all the time.*

But Tila also felt guilty for pushing him. Malachi was clever in a way most people could never be. She had seen him find solutions to problems that even confounded Theo, but he never claimed any credit for himself. He seemed to enjoy being a cog in a machine, just one part among many.

She realised then that she didn't need Theo's help with this data chip. She trusted Malachi. He knew as much as anyone else.

More, probably.

A soft chime from the workbench brought the present into focus. She fetched a spare stool and dragged it across the workshop to sit next to the others. The metal feet shrieked horribly against the floor and made Ellie shudder as the noise scraped its nails up her spine and dug into her brain.

Malachi was rapidly entering commands into the computer without looking at the keys. He pressed a button and the screen filled with what seemed to be a random mix of numbers, letters, and symbols. He rubbed his tired eyes and blinked.

"Have you slept?" Tila asked. "You look exhausted."

"A bit. The encryption on the chip was stronger than I thought. It took me some time."

"How much time?"

"All night."

"What? Why?"

"I was just trying to help."

"And you never met a problem you couldn't solve," Ellie said. "He hates letting a machine get the better of him," she added.

Tila pointed at the meaningless data on the screen. "Is that the chip? Do you know what it does?"

"I do now. This chip bridges the communication and navigation systems. You're looking at the raw data, though. Let me fix it for you so it makes sense."

He entered more commands, and the display changed into four neat columns. The first was a long block of numbers. The second column was a short alphanumeric sequence. The third was mostly blank but some rows displayed a two-digit number. The final column was another long string of numbers.

"Oh good. That makes sense," said Ellie flatly.

Malachi held up a finger. "Wait, I can parse it in more detail."

Ellie looked over at Tila with raised eyebrows. Tila shrugged a reply. Neither of them spoke the same language as Malachi.

"Got it," said Malachi proudly, "That's much better."

Tila disagreed. The only difference she could see was that the first column of numbers was now separated with periods, and the last column was separated with dashes.

"Is it?" she asked doubtfully.

"Sure it is! Look here." He pointed at the first column. "This here is a timecode sequence. It's coded in local time here but I can convert it to interstellar standard. The second column is the hex-code for the address of the transmission. The third column is a Jump ID signature. That only appears when Jump data is being coordinated among the ships who are about to take part. The last column is the local ship's VOP."

Ellie poked him in the ribs. "Are you going to make us ask you what that means?"

"It's the only way you'll learn. It's the Velocity, Orientation and Position of a ship. It's important for ships to know to make a smooth Jump but I don't think it's relevant here."

"So, no messages?" Tila said. Her heart sank.

Peter A Dixon

"No. This is Jump metadata, not communications, but we were lucky to find it."

"Why? If we don't have the messages I don't see how any of this helps us. We still don't know any more than we did yesterday!"

Malachi tapped the first column of numbers on the screen. "But we do," he said. "We might not have any messages, but what we do have is a complete log of ship transmissions for a fleet Jump."

He waited.

"And?" said Tila.

"And, anytime more than one ship is involved in a Jump, each navigation system has to synchronize with the rest of the flight group. It ensures all the relevant details are included in the point of origin calculation. It's usually the pilot's job to authorize these transmissions, but if a ship is regularly part of the same Jump group or docked inside a larger ship, like this one probably was, it's easier just to leave the systems on automatic."

"I hate using automatics," said Ellie, "I always forget how they are supposed to work."

"Ok, so what does this actually tell us?" Tila asked, annoyed by Ellie's interruption.

Malachi tapped the first column again. "This is the big one. These entries are the timestamps of the system messages so from

157

this we can tell when the messages were sent. Do you want to have a guess how far they go back?"

Tila shook her head. "How far?"

"Twelve years. In fact, the earliest one dates to twenty-four hours before the colony Jump. I checked."

"Why would they be twenty-four hours *before*?" Ellie asked.

"It was a big mission to an unknown destination. My guess is that some of this data was generated during simulated Jumps prior to the real one."

He pointed at some other entries further down the screen where the numbers were only seconds apart. "You see here how the entries become more frequent? This must be the final sequence, and this line here is the moment of the Jump."

"How can you be sure?" Tila asked cautiously as she peered closer. This was her history. If what Malachi was telling her was correct she was looking at a record of the day her parents died. It was strange to think that such a traumatic event could be recorded so dispassionately in just a few lines of code.

"After the Jump takes place nothing happens for a long time. The next entry doesn't appear until about four months later."

"Why so long?" asked Ellie.

"I don't know. The colonists would have had to wait at least a couple of weeks before making a return Jump so they could gather accurate data about the new system, data they would need for a new point of origin calculation, but in theory a return Jump would be much easier to calculate because by then they would have solid data on both sides of the equation. Four months is a long time, though."

"That's why everyone thought the *Far Horizon* was lost forever," Tila said. "They assumed that if it survived the Jump it would have sent back a ship as soon as possible."

Ellie nodded, then said, "You know we are still talking about this ship as if it is the one Tila was looking for, right?"

Malachi looked at Tila. "Well, I think it is."

Tila pushed away from the desk and paced back and forth around the workshop. "Ok, so we know, we *think*, this is from the *Far Horizon*. That means the Jump worked...," she paused. "Wait, do we know if everyone on board survived?"

"We don't have any reason to think otherwise. This hauler survived so the colony ship must have arrived safely. Besides, someone had to fly this ship back."

"Right. That makes sense." She resumed her pacing, "So we know they made it, and we know this ship came back. So where is everyone else? It's been twelve years. This can't be the only Jump home they did."

"Did they Jump back to the same system they left?" said Ellie.

Malachi shook his head. "That's something I don't know. Jump coordinates are encrypted to prevent jump-jacking. I can't reverse the hashed data to work out where they went."

"What do you mean?" asked Ellie.

Malachi tapped the controls and the display changed. The first column of timecode data was joined by two meaningless sequences of letters and numbers. He pointed at this new data. "This first column is the same timecode data as before from the day of the Jump, but now it's only showing the entries for completed Jumps. This second column is the Jump point of origin. The third column is the destination. We know the colony mission Jumped from Selah so that means that this first line of hashed coordinates must be for that star. We also know their destination, so the first entry of the third column must be for Baru. Now, the second row of data is the return journey, four months later. See how the data in the second column matches the first line in the third column? That's how I know it left from Baru. But the last entry could be anything."

"Why?" pressed Tila.

"Because there are five stars in Jump range of Baru. Selah, Berendal, Jenova, Praxis and Avion. All I know for sure is that the ships didn't return to Selah or I would have a hash match. It has to be one of the other four, but it's impossible to know which one."

"Can't you get logs from other ships that have been to those systems and compare them?" said Ellie.

"That's a really good idea, Ellie, but it's not that easy. These hashes are a combination of point of origin and point of destination. This is the only ship we know which has made a journey to and from Baru so there's nothing I can look up."

Ellie smiled at Malachi's praise.

Why can't any of this be simple? Tila thought, growing frustrated again. *One minute it was good news, then bad news again.*

"But they must have brought back the survivors to one of those systems," said Ellie, "So which one would be most likely?"

"Praxis has no inhabited planets, I think?" Tila said.

"It used to. It had asteroid mines years ago, but then there was that big battle during the war. I don't think anyone lives there now," said Malachi.

"That still leaves three systems," said Tila.

"But three of the most heavily populated systems in the Commonwealth. That's thousands of ships, and billions of people across nine planets."

"But it should be easy to find anyone that came back." said Ellie.

"So why has no one ever heard from them?" Malachi said.

None of them had an answer to this.

Unless they're hiding, thought Tila.

"I found one more thing in the data," he continued. "I don't think it helps us much, but it's, well, odd." The screen changed again to display a complex equation that looked like even more incomprehensible figures and symbols to the girls.

"What's that?" said Tila. Ellie just made a face.

Malachi tapped the screen to draw their attention to one part of the equation. "This is the Jump calculation, and this variable here represents the ship's mass. On the return Jump it's way higher than it should be."

"Compared to what?" said Ellie.

"The outbound Jump."

"More people?" said Tila.

Ellie peered at the nonsense on the screen, impressed that anyone could understand it.

Malachi shook his head. "No, it's something else. Even if it was full of people the mass reading wouldn't be this high. It's something heavy, though."

"Well you said it was a cargo ship," said Ellie. "Maybe it was cargo."

"But what cargo? And where did it go? Those haulers are for shifting things within their local system. That's why they don't have Jump engines. And what would they bring back? The colonists would need to keep anything they find to help make the mission work."

"You're giving me more questions than answers," complained Tila. "You've already told me this ship is from the colony mission. That's what I wanted to know. But all this...," she waved a hand at the screen, "this doesn't tell me what happened. It doesn't tell me where my father is."

"I know," Malachi agreed. "It's messy and confusing. But something else is bothering me."

Tila sighed. "What else?"

"Forget everything we've learned so far. We know the *Far Horizon* survived its journey and at least one ship has returned, but no one's ever heard of it. The only reason we know is because we found a ship with one chip which had been overlooked when everything else had been removed. And this ship was buried deep when most ships are integrated at the surface."

"You think someone hid the ship here?" said Ellie.

"But why?" said Tila.

"That's the real question, isn't it? 'Why?' I can only think of one reason."

Malachi took a deep breath and answered his own question. "When that colony mission failed, I don't think it was an accident."

10

The next three days passed by like treacle.

It was a quiet time in New Haven. No new ships were expected for another week, and local border issues seemed under control, so there was little work that required her help. The only novelty was the *Orion*, still under repair by Theo, and that was certainly nothing she could help with.

Tila had left Malachi's workshop more troubled than when she entered.

Malachi's conclusion thrilled and chilled her in equal measure. It meant hope, of a sort, but it was hope edged with fear and more questions. The possibilities it hinted at held a dangerous attraction.

She could easily jump to outlandish conclusions based on what Malachi had found, but if he was right then that truth demanded a response. Truth demanded that she do something, that she act, instead of remaining in this state of passive anger.

Until now, Tila had always felt she could overcome whatever life threw at her. She had done it before, many times, but this - this was something else. In the last twelve years, she had often acted rashly, often enough to have learned that the wise action was sometimes careful, but it was still action. She could still *do* something, *achieve* something. To only sit and think and wonder about the actions she did not take was something she could not do.

But there was no action she could take, and so she ached for something she could do. Something other than waiting for the enormity of their suspicion to crush her under the weight of its implications.

At times like this Tila felt the burning need to move. She could not dwell on problems. She worked through them, so she had retreated to her makeshift gym and was working out her frustrations there.

It was a spartan room, out of the way of other living quarters. It was too remote from the main population to be practical for storage or habitation. One day she would have to give it up as the population continued to grow, but for now it was her secret. Her own private get-away.

And it was perfect.

The beams and girders bracing the hull gave her somewhere to stretch and practice and train without bothering anyone and, more importantly, without anyone bothering her.

Today she needed to do something more vigorous than simply stretch. She was working out her frustrations on a makeshift punch bag.

She danced around it and punched, danced and jabbed, danced and kicked for as long as she could, until the ache in her muscles finally overtook the ache in her heart, and she could sleep.

But sleep was no willing partner tonight. Questions tumbled over in her mind, each one demanding attention and each one overtaken by the next.

How could the colony mission have been sabotaged? Who would gain and what would be their prize?

No mission of that scale had been launched in a hundred years, not since long before contact with earth had been lost.

The expense involved was, quite literally, astronomical. To construct even a single colony ship would cost tens of billions, and then there was ancillary equipment and craft to consider, as well as the crew and training required for the four thousand or so individuals on board.

And this mission wasn't taking any chances: the investors had provided enough funds and resources to build three ships.

Is Malachi asking me to believe that someone had the means and will to murder eight thousand colonists and destroy space craft worth hundreds of billions? For what? What could they possibly gain? It made no sense. Even if someone had the means to pull off a heist like this, why not steal all three ships?

What made one ship a more valuable prize than three? Was there something special about the Far Horizon?

What could someone gain that was worth so much death?

Her life had been anchored to that moment when her world had ended. She witnessed the explosion first hand, had felt and heard the terrible screams of people and tearing metal as the ships collided.

She remembered the fear and terrible dread that filled the observation room as the canopy closed, shutting out the light of the stars. It was a moment fixed in her life forever. She and too few others had lived through it.

Tila knew what happened. She knew what it meant.

Or so she thought. The data they found in the hauler had changed everything.

More questions burned in her mind. *How did the ship end up here? Who put it there? What were they trying to hide by burying it so deep?*

The rational part of her mind told her there was an explanation for everything. But another part of her sensed shadows in the darkness. Mystery and death did not easily lie together.

She was sure something underhanded must have taken place.

Be taking place? But what? And how was the colony Jump involved?

So, what am I sure of? Today, everything is different, so what do I know? I know someone hid that ship here. That means someone knows it exists. Someone knows it came back from Baru.

So, they know travel between Baru and at least one other system is possible but they're keeping it secret. Is it the same person who hid the ship in the city?

Is it even one person?

Unless Malachi could unearth any more data from the chip it would be impossible to find out. As much as she had faith in his ability to perform the impossible there were still limits to what he could do. And even if he could find out where the ship had been going, how would that information help her?

It frustrated her that she didn't have the answers. It frustrated her more that she didn't know the right questions.

She punched the bag again, a fast combination she finished with an elbow strike to an imaginary head.

Suppose they did learn where the ship had been delivering its unknown cargo. Maybe they could go there and...then what? Wait weeks, or months, for another ship to arrive?

There must be another way, she thought. *There must be something useful they can get from that stupid chip.*

That had a rhythm she could use. She repeated it to herself.

Stupid chip – jab, jab.

Stupid chip – jab, jab.

Stupid chip – jab, jab, jab, jab.

Punch.

The only useful data they had extracted was the timestamps, but what use were they, really?

They showed that the hauler had made system Jumps after the *Far Horizon* vanished, but that was all. Would anyone believe that the three of them had uncovered some great mystery based on that?

Tila paused, and leaned against the bag. But it was impossible for the hauler to have returned on its own. Malachi said it was too small to have a Jump drive so that meant at least one other ship was involved.

It felt like a step forward, but only a tiny step. After all, where was the other ship?

Did knowing that add more pieces to this puzzle, or obscure the pieces she already had?

Why had no one ever heard from the colonists?

Why discover a new star, live to tell the tale, and then keep it a secret?

Why leave two colony ships to be destroyed? That would only make things more difficult once they got to Baru. They would have only a third of the resources of the complete mission. Who would throw away so much in time and lives and money?

Who could afford to?

So many questions. But there were answers too, some brightness in the night sky. Their discovery meant her parents were *right*. It meant the Jump tech her father had developed worked, and the mission her mother led was successful. No matter what history recorded. No matter what popular opinion believed. The Jump worked. The beacon design worked and the star Baru was viable. The hauler could not have returned otherwise.

Maybe there was something she could do with that knowledge. Her parent's reputations had been vilified - no, destroyed - in the aftermath of the tragedy. They could not defend themselves, and neither could an orphaned eight-year old child. But here she had the proof they were right. And it began to dawn on her for the first time that the attacks on their character stung almost as much as their deaths.

She had seen her parents die only once but each attack, each false accusation, each lie, was like living through it all over again.

They blamed the tragedy on faulty Jump calculations, and they blamed the calculations on her father. But her father's work was right. The *Far Horizon* hauler was the proof.

Although no one had blamed her parents for the explosion aboard the *New Dawn* her mother, in her role as mission commander, had been criticised for not saving more lives. To her critics, it mattered not at all that she had lost her own life along with thousands of others in a hopeless situation. The dead can't defend themselves.

But her father had been aboard the *Far Horizon*. His ship had Jumped first. Now she had evidence it had survived.

Maybe he had survived too.

But if he was still alive why had he not returned? Why had no one been heard from since?

Someone had to pilot the cargo-hauler back and it can't have been the only ship to survive.

Some colonists had survived, at least, but where were they hiding.

What were they hiding?

Tila shook her head, flinging droplets of sweat around the room. She narrowed her eyes and punched again, and again, and again. She vented her anger in powerful strikes, yelling with each one until her back and shoulders begged her to stop.

Finally, she dropped to the floor, leaned back against the punch bag and calmed her breathing. She stretched and flexed her palms and fingers to ease the tension and cared nothing for the spots of blood seeping from her knuckles.

The realistic thing would be to assume her father was dead. Tila had heard all the scientific explanations when she was a child, although she had only come to understand them as an adult.

The Jump point was unstable and had collapsed to an infinitely small point. The shockwave would have obeyed the laws of physics and followed the direction of travel through the portal.

The deadly blast of energy on the far side of the wormhole would have devastated any ships to close to the event horizon.

The *Far Horizon* would have been caught in the blast. Crew occupying the inner compartments might have survived the initial blast because of the extra layers of shielding. But the system damage would be critical. Power and life support would have died, and so, a short time later, would the crew.

But anyone in the outer hull, such as the bridge, such as her father, would have been killed instantly by the high-energy particle blast.

Painlessly, they told her.

And he never came back. That was all the proof she needed.

Tila twisted her head from side to side, stretching neck muscles, keeping herself supple and moving, and knowing what would happen if she stayed still for too long.

So, some things can't be changed, but what can I do with what I know? Does anyone even still care? It happened so long ago. It's not like anyone still has a stake in a mission that took place more than ten years ago, is it?

Is it?

No, that's not right. Someone would want to know. People invested money in the mission. Rich, powerful people. It was too big for any government to fund alone. Those investors would want to know the truth. Wouldn't they?

Corporations go to court all the time to reclaim investments gone bad. Maybe to the right investors this knowledge was worth something, and maybe they would be able to redeem her parent's reputation and make it known that they did nothing wrong. The accident wasn't their fault. The mission should have been a success.

She remembered the ship they found, and the data within.

It was a success.

Everyone involved in the mission, everyone who had a stake in its outcome - investors, survivors and investigators - wanted someone to blame. After the accident, everyone had wanted someone to blame. What could be more human than that? But Tila had always known they had blamed the wrong people. Now she could prove it. The people behind this, those who truly deserved the blame for lies, theft and murder, were still out there somewhere, hiding around a distant star.

Tila felt lighter now, and the fog inside her head was clearing. She hated being aimless. She had always wanted hope, but now more than hope she needed a plan. Needed focus.

Finally, she had all three.

It was settled then. She would find the investors who funded the colony mission and tell them what she knew. The data chip would prove her claims.

The investors, in their gratitude, would use their vast resources to investigate further.

And maybe, eventually, she could vindicate her parent's memories and make sure history knew they were not failures.

It wasn't much, but it was a plan.

All she needed now was a ship.

11

Malachi's ship was broken, and he didn't know why.

He lay on his back, underneath the raised body of the *Rhino*, making silent threats to a machine that refused to listen.

Holding a hatch open with one hand, Malachi scrabbled with the other until his fingers touched a wire. He tugged it closer until he could reach the infrasound probe attached to the other end. He switched it on and hurried to complete the job before the inaudible tone made him nauseous.

"Is it fixed yet?" asked a familiar voice.

He shut off the tool, grateful for the interruption, and slid himself out to see Tila's upside-down face studying the diagnostic equipment. She offered her hand.

"It's not broken, it's just not working," he said. He took her hand and pulled himself to his feet. "Where have you been? Ellie's worried about you."

"She worries too much. I'm fine."

"Are you?"

"I am now. I know what we need to do."

Malachi wiped the worst of the dirt from his hands and dragged over two stools so they could sit. "Tell me."

She took a breath, anticipating his likely reaction. "We need to find the investors in the mission and tell them what we know."

Malachi blinked. "That's your plan? Ok! Firstly, 'we'? Second, what will they do about it? Why should they even believe you? And third, how are you even going to find them?"

"Firstly, yes. Second, we can take the chip you found, that's our proof. They'll have to believe that, won't they?"

Her eyes told him she needed them to believe that.

"Look, I agree that the only explanation for that data is because a ship made the Jump back from Baru, but who's going to listen to us? We're nobodies. Who are these investors, and how do we get to meet them, anyway?"

"But we're nobodies who know something. Plus, I'm the daughter of the people who led

178

the mission. That has to count for something, right?"

"How can you make them believe that? You could be anyone claiming a story like that. They won't have any reason to believe us, uh, you."

He was right, she realised. Her word alone would not carry any weight. "So, is that it? Are you saying it won't work?"

"No. I'm... I'm just saying it might be harder than you think. Let's start at the beginning. Which investors do we talk to?"

"I don't know. I hoped you might."

"Me? What do I know about stuff like that? I build and fix things."

"But you have access to data, don't you? What happened is public record, so it should be on the networks."

"Public records in one star system don't automatically appear in another, and hardly anything useful turns up here," he mused. "On the other hand, the mission was a long time ago and a big event, so there is probably something we can find on local archives. Even the Juggernaut gets news eventually, right? Let me have a look."

Malachi turned to one of his computers and began searching for the old records of the colony mission.

Tila, for once, waited patiently.

"Ok, here's something. A big chunk of the mission was funded by a cabal of investors from the three closest systems; Selah, Kinebar and Jenova. Most of the rest came from Avion, and some of the smaller systems. That makes sense. No one wants to come via our system if they can help it. Baru would have given them an alternate route. It might not make journeys any quicker but it would make them cheaper."

"Because the traders wouldn't have to pay for protection against the pirates?"

"Right. Plus, Baru might give them more trading opportunities. There's nothing in our system except what we are hiding in the Juggernaut, and who want's that? Anyway, it looks like most of the investment came from corporations based on Parador, in the Jenova system."

"Jenova? I thought Selah was the richest system."

"It is, but most of the big corporations started in Jenova and expanded to Selah later. Selah is where they make their money, but Jenova is where the power is."

"So, where do we go?"

Malachi drummed his fingers on the workbench as he considered the question. "I think we should try Jenova. That's where the decisions are made."

"Ok!" Tila hugged him in a moment of rare delight. "So we're going to Parador! Thank you!"

"Tila, this isn't going to be easy. These are powerful and important people. You can't count on just turning up and expect them to listen to you."

"I can make them listen."

Malachi shook his head and spun his chair so they were face to face. "No, you can't, Tila. You can't barge in and expect people to listen. You can't just act without consequence there. It's not like the *Juggernaut*. Here it's uncivilised and dangerous and you have to be strong to survive, but life planet-side is nothing like this. They have governments and police and bodyguards and security forces and laws. All of the corporations will have their own private security forces too, so if you get angry, or aggressive, they will just throw you out or lock you up."

"It's not my first time on a planet, you know. I'm not Ellie."

"I know that, but you've lived here for too long. Don't forget what it's like. I'm just saying you can't act there like you do here. You have to be careful. We need to be more diplomatic."

"So, you do think it's hopeless."

"I didn't say that, I just don't think it will be easy. You can't just fight your way in to get someone's attention."

"You mean *I* need to be more diplomatic, don't you?"

"Well, yes."

Tila fell silent for a moment. "That was a very diplomatic way of putting that, by the way. It's a good thing you're coming with me."

"Me? What makes you so sure I'm going?"

"Going where?" asked Ellie as she bounced into the room unannounced.

"Nothing," said Tila quickly at the same time that Malachi said, "Parador."

"What? We are? Why? Parador? Wait, what do you mean nothing?" she said to Tila.

Tila threw Malachi a scowl. "He meant me and him," she said.

"Why can't I come?" whined Ellie.

"It's not that we don't want you to," said Tila quickly in an attempt to smooth things over, "But we'll only be gone a few days, and it will be boring. I'm going to try to meet the investors in the colony mission and tell them what we found."

"Boring!? Are you joking? You're leaving here without me and going to a planet and you think I'm going to find that *boring*? How could you think that?"

"It will only be for a couple of days-" Tila started to say.

"I don't care if it's for a couple of minutes! How could you leave me behind? You know I've never been on a planet! It's because you two talk about the things you remember from growing up on a world and I don't know what any of them are. That's it, isn't it?" she accused.

"No, of course not!" Tila protested, "I-"

Ellie turned on Malachi. "And we were only talking the other day about how much you said I would enjoy flying through clouds instead of space."

Malachi pointed an accusing finger at Tila. "Hey, I didn't say you couldn't come!"

Ellie threw up her hands. "Of course I'm coming! Someone has to look after you two. Malachi will be hopeless, just like he always is when he is not working on some machine, and you, Tila, need someone to keep an eye on you to stop you getting into trouble."

She put her hands on her hips and stared them down. Malachi and Tila looked at each other. It was not often Tila lost a fight but Malachi had the feeling that this one was over before it began.

"Fine," said Tila eventually, giving up.

"Great," said Malachi, "And I'm not hopeless."

"Perfect," said Ellie, "When are we leaving?"

"Well, I need to finish getting the ship ready-"

"Your dad's letting you take his ship?"

Malachi's expression was all Ellie needed to realise this was not, in fact, the case.

"Oh! He's not? That will be...interesting when he finds out."

Malachi looked at Tila. "She's got a point. It's not like my dad's just going to let us take the *Rhino*."

"So don't tell him. He sometimes leaves the system on business, doesn't he? Does he ever go to Parador?"

Malachi thought about this. "Not if he can help it. He avoids the whole system if he can. He might have been to Mirador but I'm sure he hasn't been to Parador."

"But you can still get us the ship, right?" Tila pressed.

"Maybe. But what about the port fees when we get there? They won't be cheap. And the toll for the Jump, and fuel costs, and-"

"One problem at a time," she assured him.

Tila had made her decision. She was going to Parador.

12

Tila spent the rest of the day in the workshop at Malachi's computer becoming increasingly irritable as the day dragged on.

The archived news that she uncovered emphasised the spectacle of the adventure of the colony mission and the pioneer spirit of the volunteer colonists.

Most of the stories avoided dry details like the complex web of funding for the mission made between dozens of corporations across multiple star-systems. It was all fluff and no substance.

I thought computers were supposed to make this easier.

Tila didn't doubt that Malachi could have found the information she sought in a fraction of the time, but she was already asking a lot of him.

Getting the ship wasn't going to be easy. Without an airtight reason Theo would have no reason to let his son leave the system, and there was no need to complicate things by telling Theo that Ellie and Tila would also be coming. Some things were best left unsaid to Theo as far as Tila was concerned.

But should Ellie come?

Tila needed Malachi. Although she didn't expect the trip to be dangerous, she was grateful that he was capable enough to look after himself.

Ellie, on the other hand, was neither of those things. Sure, if they needed someone to flash a smile and look pretty Ellie would be her first choice, but otherwise she would just be in the way, wouldn't she?

Do I want to spend the whole trip worrying about Ellie when I have something this important to do?

Tila grunted to herself as she read and made notes, annoyed that Ellie was distracting her already and they hadn't even left yet. How bad would it be when they arrived?

Maybe it was for the best that Ellie stayed behind.

Tila tried to concentrate once more on the task at hand, when Ellie suddenly arrived in person, bounded into the room and shrieked that Malachi was chasing her with dirty hands.

"Tila, help me!" she squealed. Ellie leapt behind Tila to use her as a human shield. Ellie bumped against the chair as she turned and accidentally nudged Tila's elbow. Tila's hand stumbled against the keyboard and erased the work of the last twenty minutes.

Malachi ambled in. He was filthy, with black stains covering his already dark skin and most of his clothing.

"I told you it wasn't going to work!" He pointed a playfully accusing finger at Ellie.

"I didn't make you do it!" Ellie protested.

"It was better to take the chance than listen to you keep badgering me about it."

"Hey!" shouted Tila, "What's going on?"

"*Somebody*, thought it would be a good idea to drain the lubricant from her racer without depressurizing the system," said Malachi.

"Well *somebody* who is an engineer should know better than to listen to my advice," countered Ellie.

"I was trying to save time so you would stop nagging me."

"I don't nag!"

"You haven't stopped all day!"

"HEY!" Tila slammed her hand down on the table. Couldn't they see that she was trying to work? "Do you have to do that in here?"

Ellie and Malachi exchanged a glance.

"Sorry, Tila," said Malachi, his smile fading, "But I need a detergent from the stores. It's the only thing that gets this dirt out."

He shrugged at Ellie behind Tila's back and began searching through storage boxes for the cloths and sprays he needed. As far as he was concerned that was the end of it.

As far as Ellie was concerned it was not. "What's your problem?" she demanded, turning on Tila. "We're only trying to get ready for a race."

"I'm busy!"

"Why does that mean I can't have any fun?"

"Because things are not always fun, ok? Sometimes we have to do things that we don't enjoy because they need to be done."

"So, if you're not happy then no one else can be happy? Is that it?"

"That's not fair."

"It's not fair that we have to be miserable around you all the time."

"I'm concentrating."

"You're never happy."

"Hey! I never said you have to be miserable, but you don't have to be so over-excited all the time either. I'm going to Parador for a reason. It's not going to be a game, or another race. It's serious."

188

"So why can't I be excited to go with you? It doesn't mean I'm not taking it seriously."

"You could try acting like it for once," Tila snapped.

"You could try smiling! I thought we found something that would cheer you up, but you're moodier than ever!"

"Hope always lets you down. If you grew up you'd understand that."

Ellie flinched at that comment, and Tila was ashamed that it pleased her. She turned back to the computer and tried to retrieve the work she had just lost.

Ellie took a breath and counted to five in her head to keep her temper in check before she spoke again. "I'm here for you, Tila. We both are. And we both know what this means to you, but that doesn't mean we have to mope around when we come."

"Well, I'm not asking you to come!" Tila yelled, exasperated, and immediately regretted losing her temper when she saw the hurt in Ellie's eyes.

They both fell silent, holding each other's gaze, each of them frustrated and infuriated by the intransigence of the other. They searched each other's eyes for a glimmer of understanding or sympathy, but if it was there, neither of them could find it.

Malachi decided the wisest thing he could do was to say nothing.

"Ok. Fine," said Ellie, without looking away, "We can talk about this later."

"Fine," said Tila, turning back to the computer. She didn't lose fights to her enemies. She wasn't going to lose one to her friend.

Ellie softened first. "I'm just trying to help you Tila."

I know, thought Tila, but she said nothing.

The moment passed from hesitation to awkwardness and then to deliberate silence too quickly for Tila to make a peace offering. Ellie waited for Tila to say something, offer anything, that meant this barbed exchange would be relegated, like countless others before to a minor fight quickly resolved but nothing came, and Ellie's heart broke.

Without saying anything else, Ellie walked from the room.

"Who are you racing?" Tila turned quickly, but too late. Ellie was already gone.

"Good luck," Tila called after her.

"She's a little whirlwind sometimes," observed Malachi.

Tila just nodded and stared at her hands.

Malachi drummed his fingers on his seat as he watched Tila lose herself in her thoughts again. He snapped his fingers to get her attention. "OK, what's going on?"

"What do you mean?"

"What was that about? She doesn't have a problem with this but it's obvious you do. So, what is it?"

Tila leaned back in her chair and stretched her legs. "I don't think she should come," she admitted.

"I know that. Why not? She wants to help you, just like I do. So why give her such a hard time?"

"She'll get in the way. I know she will. And I can't spend my time looking out for her. And she's too young and fluffy and-"

"Useless?" he suggested.

"I didn't say that," she objected, "But you can look after yourself. She can't. She's vulnerable when she's alone."

"She won't be alone. She'll be with us the whole time."

"What if something happens?"

"Like what?"

"Like...I don't know. Anything! She's safer here. It's not that I don't want her to come but..." she trailed off. "She's safer here," she repeated.

Malachi circled the room as Tila spoke, giving her the time and space to express herself, until he faced her again. He pulled over a stool and sat down. "You underestimate her T, you always did. She's very capable. Look at the races she wins! Don't you think that takes something the others don't have?"

"Oh come on!" Tila replied with a wave of her hand, "They let her win."

Malachi sat back in surprise. "You really think that?"

"Of course they do. They let her play and race and win because they like having her around. She's cute and fluffy and harmless and…"

"And?"

"And they like having her around."

"They?"

"Boys."

"Ha! You have no idea! She might be cute and fluffy but put her in a race and she is anything but harmless. Did you know some people refuse to race her now? She's gained a reputation for being too aggressive. Don't laugh! Do you even know what her winning streak is? She hasn't lost a race in months, but you wouldn't know that because you write her off too quickly. We might not all be like you, but don't underestimate her. She can out-fly anyone."

"Ok, so she's a good pilot. Whatever. How will that help me on Parador? We're only travelling there and back. There won't be anything for her to do!"

"I thought you said she was safe here because you didn't know what was going to happen?"

"Don't turn this around! I'm just trying to keep her from getting hurt. Look, I'm not saying she's useless but she won't be any help."

"But she *wants* to help. I don't know why you can't see that, or why that's not enough for you. She wants to help you because she cares about you. This is about looking for your family, well you're the closest thing to family she has, and honestly the irony of you trying to mother her now, of all times, is hilarious."

"She just wants an adventure."

"Tila, I want the adventure! I'm getting out of here because all I do is work and build and fix things and do what my dad tells me to do. I don't mind that, really, I don't. I enjoy it. But I want there to be more to my life than just work. I'm not going to get a chance like this again anytime soon, and I'm going to be in so much trouble when we get back my life won't be worth living. This little jaunt of yours is an excuse for me to do something I could never do alone. But Ellie? She just wants to help you.

She cares about you. Isn't that enough? Be humble enough to accept what she can offer, even if her company is all she can give."

Tila stared at him as she thought this through. "Let me get this straight. You don't really want to help me but you're using me as an excuse to get out of here?"

"Absolutely." He tried to keep his expression serious and concerned but failed and broke into a grin.

"Good. As long as we understand each other." She stood and offered him her arm which he took and stood next to her. "So, what now?" she asked him.

"Now," he replied, wandering over to the *Rhino* and giving it a kick, "We have to borrow this ship."

"First you have to fix it," Tila pointed out.

Malachi pointed at the doorway through which Ellie had fled. "Deal. I'll fix this if you go and fix that," he said.

13

Making the *Rhino* space-worthy again was the easy part.

Once Malachi had isolated the problem, he set to work sourcing the components which needed replacing and fabricating anything he couldn't find. When all else failed, he would even stoop so low as to improvise.

Malachi hated improvising. Machines were built to a plan and to strict specifications. They obeyed strict rules. They worked in a particular way - the *right* way - and it was wrong to ignore the original design and take it upon himself to make them work in some other way.

He could do it, but he hated it. He felt he was disrespecting the original engineering.

Of course, life on the Juggernaut rarely involved the luxury of having everything he needed, whether that was something as mundanely essential as a water-reclamation system, or an energy distributor for a shuttle that was already thirty years out of date when they bought it.

But necessity, as they say, is the mother of invention, or in this case improvisation. So, Malachi put his personal feelings aside and set to work.

Once the *Rhino* had been repaired, he set about overcoming the next obstacle. How could they leave the system without a Jump engine, or the money to pay the surrogate fees?

They had few options available to them, and not enough money.

The criminal option was of course the cheapest option. Hijacking a ship in transit through the Celato system was out of the question. None of them had the experience or resources necessary for an operation like that, and of course, none of them had the will or inclination to perform such a blatantly criminal act.

Malachi was already nervous about the journey, and no matter how much he claimed to be excited by the opportunity he knew the risks were real.

They could attempt to Jump-jack a departing ship, but that was also illegal and they would be reported for their crimes as soon as they reached their destination. They wouldn't get close to the atmosphere of Parador if they did that.

They could try slipstreaming another ship as it entered the portal. The penalties for this were less severe, but there would still be consequences. The change in mass at the last minute would upset the Jump calculations. To keep the equation balanced a random factor would be introduced and that meant on arrival either their destination, velocity or vector would be unknown.

If they were very unlucky all three would be randomised. The results wouldn't kill them, but there was no guarantee they wouldn't end up heading away from Parador so fast it would take them a week to turn around.

Malachi was no pirate, he had no stolen ID codes, and he had no intention of risking an approximate calculation.

Their only real option was the legal one. They would have to buy passage alongside a Jump-capable ship travelling to Jenova. This option had the welcome upside that no one would shoot them. The downside was that to buy their way out they would need money.

A lot of money.

And unfortunately for Malachi he knew only one place on the Juggernaut where he could get some.

14

When Malachi arrived at the Solarium he saw Nina was already waiting for him.

She sat on the floor by the panoramic window hugging her knees and staring at the huge red star as it began to dip below the horizon of the window.

"Almost makes you feel like you're planetside again," said Malachi, and sat down beside Nina.

She smiled without looking at him. "Almost. It's the sunsets I miss most. The only colours out there are black and red."

"It's still one more than we have in here."

"What, you don't like our fine selection of grey metal?" She looked at him for the first time, still smiling, and the sunset faded into nothing.

She handed him a data chip. "I looked at it, and I had one of my guys take a look too, but we couldn't get anything more out of it. It's encrypted with something we haven't seen before."

"Too old?"

"Too new. And probably custom code written for the colony mission. Do you want to guess how many colony ships from that expedition we have had pass through here in the last twelve years? That will tell you how much experience we have with it."

"Zero."

"Zero," she repeated. "Or maybe one. Tila might be right."

"I know. That's what I'm afraid of."

Nina gasped in mock horror. "Big strong Malachi is afraid of something?"

"Be serious. I'm afraid she will hope for something that can't be real, and that will only hurt her more."

"You care about her?"

"Of course."

"I knew it!"

"As a friend."

"Just a friend?"

"Yes."

"Good." Nina turned back to the sunset. The thin crescent of the star rested on the lower frame of the window and cast long shadows on the ceiling of the Solarium. "So, what's the plan to make sure Tila stays happy?"

"What's that supposed to mean?"

"She's always sulking about something. You and Ellie are always trying to make her happy."

"She's our friend."

"She's trouble. She's always looking for risks. I don't want her to lead you into trouble too."

"What trouble could there be on Parador?"

"I don't know, but believe me, if it's there she'll find it."

"She's not that bad."

"I don't want to talk about her anymore."

"Fine. We just want to help her, that's all."

"Don't you want to make anyone else happy?"

"Like who?"

Nina chewed her lip. "Never mind. What's your plan?"

"We're going to Parador."

"You're nuts!"

"Tila thinks she can find the people who invested in the original mission. She thinks they will want to hear what we've found."

"What you found?"

"Sorry. What you found."

"Thank you. So, how to intend to make this plan happen."

"I need a ship. And money."

"You can fix up the *Rhino*. And how much is Theo getting for the *Orion* job?"

"I fixed it, but I can't use the *Rhino*. My dad needs it for his work here."

"Then you can't go."

"You're not helping," Malachi sighed.

"I'm showing you your options."

"I don't have any options."

"You have one option."

"There's no other ships."

"Then you know what you have to do."

"He'll kill me when he finds out."

"Malachi, you can work this out. This is what you do. It's just another engineering problem to solve. You have parts that don't fit and you need to make everything work, but you can't do it if you play by the rules."

"But the rules are important. The rules are how things are supposed to work."

"Not this time. If you really want to help her then this time you need to break the rules."

"And what about money?"

"Surely Theo would have had the *Orion* pay something in advance?"

"Yeah, he did."

"There you go. Transfer that to a credit chip."

"I can't steal it!"

"I never said you didn't have to pay him back."

"My dad will kill me."

"I'll kiss it better."

"Really?"

"Sure. That's not enough incentive?"

"I don't know..."

"I do." Nina climbed to her feet and stretched her legs.

Malachi sighed again. The last of the sun vanished below the artificial horizon of the Solarium, and behind him lights began to glow.

"Are you sure you don't want to come?"

"Oh, I'm very sure! Parador is not the place for me. One day you can take me to Peleg. I want to look at the stars there and try and find earth. You can bring me back a souvenir though.

"What do you want?"

"What does any girl want, Malachi? I want to go back to my old life, away from this place."

"I don't think I can do that."

"Surprise me then. Make me feel special."

"How?"

Nina stretched one last time and stood up to leave. "Easy. Bring me something no other girl on the Juggernaut has."

Malachi thought about this. "Like what?" he asked as she walked away.

"You like solving problems, Malachi. You figure it out."

15

Malachi stopped short of the door to his father's tiny office and took a moment to work up the courage to enter.

Act natural. We've run short of parts before. The voice in his head reassured him. *It's nothing unusual.*

Then, as ready as he could be, he stepped into the room as if it was any other day.

Theo sat behind his desk. It was a simple metal sheet propped up by the landing struts they had removed from the *Rhino*.

Malachi felt like his father already knew the lie he was about to hear.

I've interrupted him. This is a bad time.

The room was dimmer than the last time Malachi had been here. Colder too. His father must have passed on the light panel they had salvaged last week. Most likely his father had added it to the lottery pool rather than keeping it for himself.

Despite his skills and position, Theo considered himself last in the queue for essential items such as lights. Far better, he would explain, that the rest of New Haven is well lit. The light makes people feel safer, and danger more easily hides in the shadows than in the sun.

Theo placed his data pad on his desk and gave his son, as he did everyone he spoke with, his full attention. "What is it, Malachi?"

"I know you're busy..." Malachi began.
Theo smiled. In here, working alone, he could devote himself to one problem after another until he was satisfied he could resolve each one in turn. Away from his desk he had to juggle a hundred demands at once. Here, without the stress that came from dealing with people, he could almost relax.

"I'm always busy, so now is as good a time as any. What's the problem, son?" There had to be a problem. Malachi did not interrupt his work without good reason.

Keep it simple.

"I was checking our inventory. I think I found a problem."

"I thought we weren't due to audit our inventory for another two weeks."

Uh oh.

"Uh, I wanted to make sure we had enough essentials in stock, you know, because of the work you've been doing on the *Orion*."

Theo considered his son thoughtfully as he leaned forward over his desk.

He's not buying it!

"You know," said Theo, "The last audit was only three weeks ago. Based on that I have everything I need to repair the *Orion*'s engine core, but with everything else happening around here I didn't think to check again. I should have. Good thinking. So, what's the problem?"

We have plenty of gear to fix an engine, even one that badly designed. Why didn't I think of that?

"I was, uh, checking the lower priority stock. You know how quickly something you don't think is important can get really important fast."

You're rambling.

"Are we low on something?"

"Well, I can't find any regulators for the CO2 scrubbers in the stores."

"We have scrubbers but no regulators? How did that happen?"

Malachi shrugged so he wouldn't have to lie.

"Scrubbers without regulators are no good," said Theo. "I know that they're supposed to be independent systems but it hardly ever happens that one fails without the other."

Malachi nodded encouragingly. "I don't think any of our contacts due to deliver in the next few weeks. So, I was wondering, can we last that long? What if something breaks?"

No way will he buy that question. Of course we can't go on like this. Scrubbers might be simple tech but without a regulator in place to monitor the CO_2 build up we could all suffocate in our sleep.

"Let me check the schedules," said Theo. He poked the terminal on the side of the desk until it gave him an answer he didn't like. "You're right, this is going to be a problem." He looked up, rightly anticipating the answer to his next question. "I assume you have a solution in mind?"

"I was thinking, as you are busy with *Orion*, maybe, umm, I could go and get them?"

Pleasepleasepleasepleaseplease.

"You want me to let you take the *Rhino* and go to Selah alone?"

Malachi nodded, not trusting himself enough to speak without giving himself away.

It's not going to work. He knows. He won't let me go. He'll have another plan, he always does. He-

"Very well."

-what?

"What?" he said out loud.

"I said you can go. I won't need it for the *Orion* job. We're working in a pressurised bay and my initial investigation makes me think the problem is internal, anyway. You can be back from Selah in a couple of days."

"Jenova."

Shut up! Idiot! Say Selah. He doesn't need to know where you are really going!

"Why not Selah?"

"I need to go to Jenova. I already checked prices and reserved the items."

"You know how I feel about that system, Malachi. I avoid it whenever possible."

"I know but, but, it saves us a lot of money. And I can get what I need on Mirador."

Liar.

Theo leaned back in his chair and considered his son's proposal. He would rather Malachi travelled to Selah. It would be a longer journey. Thanks to the orbit of the city, at this time of year the Selah Beacon was located on the far side of Celato.

He had no reason to doubt Malachi was right about the price of the regulators though, and that was where they could save money. The Jump fees would be the same either way. There was no need to squander the fees from the *Orion* job. And he had to admit that the space lanes around Jenova were better patrolled than any of Selah's planets.

He knew Malachi was aware of the special risks involved in travelling near Parador but a gentle reminder would still be helpful. "Are you sure you can get what you need on Mirador?"

Malachi nodded again. Any moment now his heart was going to burst through his chest and bounce off the wall above his father's head.

"I won't need to land on Parador. The *Rhino*'s registration might still be on a watch list there. But do you really think it is? We left years ago."

Theo thought carefully before answering. His son deserved some measure of truth by now. He was a more capable and honest young man than Theo was at the same age. The whole truth could come later.

"Honestly? I don't know. But we can't risk having the ship impounded, and more importantly I can't have you caught up in any of the fallout from my past mistakes."

Malachi was taken aback by this uncharacteristic admission of a failing. His father worked so hard to avoid mistakes that it was a shock to hear him acknowledging one so large that it had forced them to leave their home. But even this was overshadowed by his father's look of concern. "Don't worry, I'll be careful."

"One more thing. I imagine that your friends would like to accompany you on this trip, especially Ellie. Can I assume you have spoken to them about this already?"

Uh-oh.

"I mentioned it."

"I don't want them to go with you. Tila will get into trouble, and Ellie is too young. She would be safer here. I don't want to be worrying about them as well as you. Understand?"

Malachi nodded. Was that a yes?

"And be careful. Don't talk to anyone you don't need to. Don't draw attention to yourself. Don't break any rules."

I wish he hadn't said that! Now I'm not only lying to him but I'm also putting myself at risk by going to the one place he wants to protect me from. I don't think I could feel worse than I do right now. I hope he never finds out about what we are about to do. I've got what I wanted, so why do I feel so bad?

But he only said, "Yeah, I understand."

16

Malachi gripped the controls tightly and braced for impact.

"*He said what?*" Tila yelled. "I don't cause trouble!"

Malachi stole a glance at Ellie, hoping to find there some support. There was none.

"Well, sometimes you sort of, maybe, find it?"

"It's called 'not being pushed around'. You should try it sometime," she shot back.

Malachi shrugged and said nothing, fully aware of the irony of Tila's demand while she was trying to push him around. He ignored her outburst and returned to the pre-flight sequence so he could ready the *Rhino* for departure. They had already moved the ship from the workshop to one of the inner bays of the space dock. Now they only had to leave the Juggernaut.

The external lights on the little spacecraft dimmed automatically as the bay doors slowly opened to reveal the main dock.

The launch bay space doors could be closed and the entire space dock pressurised if necessary, but they were usually kept open to accommodate the volume of traffic. Instead, it was the dozens of smaller docking bays which would seal and pressurize as needed.

Malachi carefully raised the *Rhino* from the platform with short, controlled bursts of the manoeuvring thrusters and guided the ship out into the main launch bay. As expected, the main doors were already open, letting in the distant light of a thousand silent stars. The serene background shifted and tilted as Malachi guided the little ship through the man-made cavern.

Beyond the space doors they saw other ships departing the bay and rising smoothly above the pock-marked surface of the city on vectors leading them toward one of the three Jump Beacons.

Further out, other ships held position, or flew slowly in close formation, as they waited for their turn to dock.

"Nothing can stop us now," said Tila, soaking up the view of an infinite expanse of stars which beckoned them forward into possibility.

A large cargo ship held position outside the launch bay doors.

"That's right," said Malachi cheerfully. The communications alert blinked for attention. Malachi opened the channel without thinking, "We'll be at Parador in no time at all," he said, and his father appeared on the screen.

Theo frowned. "Did you say Parador?" Malachi froze. "You told me you were going to Mirador," Theo said.

Ellie, out of view of the camera, piped up helpfully. "We are." Malachi frantically waved Tila away from the camera. "Ellie, is that you? What are you doing on board? Malachi, what's going on?"

"We *are* going to Mirador," Malachi tried to explain.

Tila, panicked, exclaimed from off screen. "What? We need to go to Parador. We talked about this!"

Theo cast the full force of his glare upon Malachi, who was still the only person he could see on his display. He instinctively moved his head around to try and see Tila, as if he was looking at the scene through a window instead of a camera.

"Tila, is that you? Malachi, what is going on? I gave you permission to travel to Mirador only and then to come right back. And I thought I made it very clear you were to go alone."

Malachi closed his eyes and wished he were anywhere else.

"Malachi, you will turn that ship around right now and wait on board until I get there."

Tila hit the button on the console to cancel the transmission and hissed at Malachi.

"How did we end up running into *him*? You said he wasn't going to be out on that ship until tomorrow."

Malachi opened his eyes. "He is! He was!"

"So why is he out there now getting in my way?"

"He was supposed to be working on the *Orion* today."

"That is the *Orion*!" said Ellie.

"He must have brought a test-flight forward. I didn't know he was making such good progress on the repairs!"

The communication panel lit up again, an urgent and unwelcome reminder of the furious message waiting for him.

"What do we do?" Malachi asked Tila.

"Nothing. He can't stop us now," Tila said.

"But he knows we're taking the ship to the Parador, and he knows you two are aboard when I promised him you wouldn't be. Now he knows I've lied to him he'll never trust me again. He will check the inventory when he lands and then he will find out I faked the records to get him to give me the money."

"Can he cancel our Jump permit?" Tila asked warily.

Malachi shook his head, his eyes never leaving the blank screen. His father was going to be beyond angry.

"The credit chip is pre-paid. He can't stop the money now either."

"Then we're ok? We can still go?"

The *Orion* was closer now. Theo had moved the larger vessel across the launch bay doors to block their path. A skilled pilot could still get through the small gap that remained but Theo was counting on the fact that no one would be reckless enough to try.

The *Orion* was now close enough that they could see Theo standing on the bridge watching them. Even from this distance he looked rigid with anger.

"Malachi, he's going to cut us off," Tila pleaded.

"But..."

"Please Malachi, we're so close," Ellie added. "Please?"

Malachi bit his lip as they drifted closer to the larger ship. He swallowed nervously and reached for the throttle.

For one heartbeat Tila feared he was going to slow down, reverse course and tell his father everything. If that happened she wouldn't get this chance again. No one else would trust her with a ship and a mission like this. She knew it was an insane venture, but it was still important to her.

She couldn't let it fail. Not now. She couldn't let Malachi turn the *Rhino* around. Even if he hated her forever this was something she had to do. Once they were outside the space dock they could fly away while she convinced him. If the *Orion* shut off their exit they would lose all the momentum which had brought them to this point. Theo would lecture Malachi, Malachi would cave, and Tila would have to give up her plan.

Tila didn't like giving up.

"It's now or never, Mal."

She inched forward, looking for her chance take the throttle and the decision out of Malachi's hands.

He will hate me forever but at least this way it will be my fault, not his. Some comfort.

She grabbed the throttle at the same moment as Malachi. They locked eyes. Tila demanding. Malachi unsure.

Then Ellie's hand appeared between them. She clamped her fingers over both their hands hand and shoved it forward, opening the throttle to full power.

The engines sprang to life, the *Rhino* surged forward, and they flashed past the *Orion*. The last thing they saw of Theo was his shocked expression blurring with speed.

"We're going!" she stated in an uncharacteristically firm tone which said 'don't argue'.

They both stared at her, mouths open.

"Woooooo?" she added.

17

Tila fell back in to her seat and shut her eyes. She opened them again slowly, afraid to look in case she discovered that what had just happened had not really happened. The air escaped her lungs in a rush. She didn't realise she was holding her breath.

Malachi stared at the stars before them with a wide eyed stunned expression. He seemed transfixed by the view. He had paled, not at the closeness of their escape but at the sure knowledge that he was going to have to return and explain himself.

Only Ellie seemed energised by the start of their adventure. "That was easy!" she said.

Malachi made a small choking noise. "Easy?"

"Don't worry Mal," she said, patting him on the head. "We can tell everyone I made you do it."

"How could you make me? You're the least frightening thing I know."

"I can be scary!"

Tila smiled at the thought of Ellie being able to frighten anyone.

"No, Ellie, you can't," she said, "But that's okay."

"I can be if I want to be," Ellie muttered and dropped herself into the centre seat.

"Now all we have to do is get to the Jump point," said Malachi.

"So, it's over?" said Ellie.

"Almost. The hard work is done. Things should be easier now, assuming we can find Tila's cabal of investors."

Ellie leaned forward on the console and looked out at the stars. As excited as she was walk on a planet for the first time this was what she lived for; the eternal magnificence of the infinite night.

"How long does a Jump take, anyway?" she asked.

"Exactly?" said Malachi.

"Sure."

"Fourteen minutes and three seconds."

"She said 'exactly', Mal." said Tila.

Ellie sprawled over the star chart in the console's central display. Her head was propped up on one hand with her fingers buried beneath blonde hair She swept her other arm across the screen until she found what she was looking for. She planted a finger on their destination and facts and figures about Jenova began popping up on the display. She examined the screen.

"So even though Jenova is sixteen light years from here it will only take fourteen minutes?"

"And three seconds. That's right."

"That's quite fast, isn't it?"

"Umm...yes."

Ellie touched another star in the opposite heading. "And what about this one, Selah. That's twenty light years away. That takes fourteen minutes too?"

"And three seconds, yes."

"So, would it take twenty-eight minutes and six seconds from Jenova to Selah?"

"No, fourteen minutes."

"And three seconds?" offered Tila.

Ellie sat up. "That makes no sense, Malachi."

"It's weird, I know, but that's how it works. It doesn't matter how far you go. It always takes fourteen minutes and three seconds."

"But it's nearly twice as far! Are you sure?"

"That's hyperspace physics for you, Ellie. It's just how it works."

"So even if we went here," she picked a star at random, a white dwarf two hundred light years away, "It would still take fourteen minutes?"

"And three seconds. Although we couldn't make it that far, anyway. Once you start trying to Jump more than twenty-five light years, even with a Beacon, the math becomes almost impossible. There's no telling where you might end up."

"How do you understand all this and still have room in your brain for everything else you know?" Tila asked.

"I'm an engineer, not an expert in hyper-space physics. I don't understand this, not really. That's just the basics everyone knows." He looked up. "Don't they?" he asked seriously.

Tila and Ellie exchanged a look.

"Yeah," said Tila.

"Sure," said Ellie. "Of course."

"Hmmm," said Malachi.

"So how far away is the Beacon for Jenova?" Ellie asked as she flicked through different screen displays.

"Not far at this time of year. Only a couple of hours."

"Two hours? Why didn't they build it closer?"

"Ellie, the Juggernaut orbits Celato. The distance changes all the time. You're lucky it's not a couple of days. Anyway, it's as close as it can be. Beacons can't be too far inside a star's gravity well or they won't work properly. Luckily, we have no planets so they built it closer."

"Why does the star make a difference?"

Smiling, Tila leaned over Ellie's ear while Malachi wasn't looking. "Here comes the lesson," she whispered.

"I heard that. Because the gravity well of star or planet is so massive that Jump Beacons can't operate too far inside a system. Well, they can, but the Jumps become more dangerous. It's easy around Celato because the Juggernaut is pretty much the only thing in this system. Think of the star like the middle of a giant whirlpool. Around Celato there is nothing to disturb the whirlpool except the Juggernaut and a few asteroids and comets. In other systems, each planet is trying to make its own little whirlpool of gravity. All those whirlpools overlap with each other and with their star, and that creates a disturbance in the uh, water."

"Does Ellie even know what a whirlpool is?" said Tila.

"I know! I've read books. Just because I grew up in space it doesn't mean I don't know anything," Ellie protested, then to Malachi she said, "So, it's sort of like 'space-water'?" said Ellie.

"I guess," said Malachi.

Tila patted Ellie on the shoulder. "He's good with the science but bad with the metaphors," she said.

"He's not that bad. It makes sense to me now," said Ellie. "There's nothing in our system so it's like a smooth pond, but other systems have planets spinning in all directions so it's harder to find somewhere to make a landing because the gravity is disturbing the space-water?"

"Uh...actually, that's pretty good," Malachi admitted.

"Is it called a gravity well because of the space-water?" asked Ellie.

"Not quite, El,"

"So, you *do* understand everything about Jump Beacons too," Tila said playfully.

"No, this is still only the basics. But you know that already, don't you?"

Tila and Ellie looked at each other.

"Yeah," said Tila.

"Sure," said Ellie. "Of course."

18

The relatively short journey meant the risk of pirate attacks was minimal, and for once the limited value of their ship also counted in their favour. It was strange how something so prized inside the city was worth so little in open space.

The rest of the flight to the Beacon was uneventful, even if Ellie considered sitting still the worst possible way to spend two hours of her life.

It was a pause for breath between the thrill of the escape and the anticipation of the unknown still to come.

Thirty minutes out from their destination they intercepted other ships travelling from the Kinebar Beacon. Together they formed a rag-tag caravan that stretched through space.

Far behind them the Juggernaut had become only a dark spot transiting the large red orb of the sun.

Identity codes and flight vectors of nearby craft popped up and vanished again on the navigational display before Malachi as ships entered and left the boundary of the *Rhino*'s short range sensors.

The display became steadily more crowded as they approached the Jenova Beacon.

As it came into range a tight cluster of blips appeared on their scanner and began to dissipate at once. A Jump group had just arrived. The cluster split into two smaller groups of ships like a cell dividing. Each small fleet began the slow transit across the solar system to one of the other Beacons where they would continue to Selah or Kinebar, and then to who knew where.

None of the arriving ships headed for the Juggernaut.

Their own passage had already been arranged. Before they had left the city, Malachi had checked for traffic scheduled for Jenova and paid the required fees. The common-law of space travel was that no ship should refuse to provide support to any needy traveller. So, while the fees were expensive they were not crippling. The laws of supply and demand were

in effect in deep space just as they were anywhere else.

Fortunately, the Juggernaut was a well-trav-
elled, if not well-loved, system, so there was
rarely any problem in finding a Jump-capable
ship willing to assist. Everyone understood the
desire to leave.

For now, he busied himself in the final preparations as Ellie gawped at the surrounding
traffic. Tila sat alone in the rear cabin, anticipation gnawing at her insides.

This is it, she thought as the Jump Beacon
announced itself to their ship's systems, *this is
when it becomes real.*

The last few days had been anything but. In
that time, her worldview had been turned upside down. Things of which she had once been
sure had been brought into question, and now,
in the moments before they left the system,
this whole adventure felt real for the first time.

She wondered again if it might have been
better to take this journey alone. Malachi was
risking a great deal by coming. She knew his
help was going come with a price, not only in
terms of his father's disappointment and anger, but also in real money – money he needed
to keep the business alive and the family fed.

The impact on his father's political reputation within New Haven would also be significant. Malachi was going to have a lot to answer for when he got back.

And so am I. Theo, and everyone else, will know I'm the cause of this. But Malachi needs to go back. I don't. I'm not family. I can leave New Haven anytime I like if - no, when - it becomes too difficult for me to stay.

It wouldn't be the first time.

Am I being too selfish? Am I jeopardising his family, and Ellie's safety on nothing but a crazy plan? But then, I never asked him or Ellie to come. Ellie just wants to come for the adventure, I guess. Just a few days on a planet, and then home again. It's not much time. I hope she loves it. There's something about the open sky which people who have spent their whole life among the stars can find unsettling. Maybe she will be like that. I hope not. I don't need her crying to go back home before I finish what I set out to do.

Maybe she shouldn't have come. She's just going to get in the way, I know it.

When Tila emerged from her thoughts they were almost at the Beacon.

Twenty kilometres in front of them one of the four vertex satellites drifted across their view in its perfect orbit. Each satellite formed one point of a precise four-sided pyramid. At the centre of the pyramid was the Nexus Beacon, the powerful supercomputer which coordinated and controlled each Jump.

Each vertex satellite was exactly one hundred kilometres away from its closest neighbour, and the whole geometric arrangement spun slowly on all three axes around the nexus.

Above them five small craft were forming up around their surrogate, a cargo ship named *Neptune's Pearl*. It was the same ship they had paid to be their own surrogate.

Malachi responded to queries and instructions sent by the *Pearl* and carefully manoeuvred the *Rhino* into its designated position within the formation.

Each ship hugged as close to the *Pearl* as possible to minimize the fleet's mass radius.

Finally, he tapped a control to transmit their ready status and sat bolt upright in his chair, tensed and waiting for the Jump.

Slowly, moving as if a single ship, the tight formation approached their departure point.

"We're locked into their Jump calculations and slaved our manoeuvring systems to theirs," he informed the girls. "Now we wait."

They didn't wait long.

The console chirped an alarm to announce the initiation of the Jump sequence. The *Rhino* oriented itself along the vector of the *Pearl*, and the little ship's engines cut automatically.

The scene around them trembled, and for the briefest of instants they had the impression of two star fields overlapping. It was like trying to focus on two different images simultaneously: one right in front of them and the other sixteen light years away.

The portal blossomed from nothing in a dazzling burst of white, tinged with red. *Neptune's Pearl* led the way and vanished from view as if it had flown into the heart of a star. The other smaller vessels raced forward and disappeared, leaving behind them a faint red afterimage.

The *Rhino* approached the event horizon. In Malachi's peripheral vision he saw the ship around him lurch awkwardly while the scene directly in front of him remained steady. He felt a twinge of motion sickness as his brain wrestled with the contradictory information being delivered by his senses. He thought Ellie might be unnerved by the effects of a Jump in a ship as small as theirs, and he had warned her what to expect ahead of time, but she didn't seem anxious at all, just excited. It was Tila who seemed tense and uncomfortable in the final moments.

Ellie sat in one of the co-pilot chairs with her feet on the controls. She couldn't remember ever feeling happier. She had left the Juggernaut for the first time. She was in a stolen ship (she told herself this made it more exciting), and she was with the two people she cared most about in the universe.

Nothing can go wrong, she thought to herself. *I hope we can find what Tila's looking for but even if we can't help her I'm going to land on a planet and look up at a sky for the first time.*

"Here we go," she whispered to herself. "Now or never."

Malachi settled back into his own chair, gripping the arm rest with his right hand so no one could see how nervous he was.

I hope I'm doing the right thing. It feels right and wrong at the same time. I've never defied my father like this, but then no one has ever needed my help like this before. This could all go wrong in a big way.

I hope this journey is worthwhile. I want Tila to find the answers she's looking for. She deserves it, if anyone does. She has the reputation of a loner but she's put her life on the line for other's before. Ellie knows that better than anyone. This is the least we can do for her.

Mostly I hope we are long gone from Parador before trouble finds us.

Tila sat in the centre chair, commanding the clearest view of the great portal which filled her horizon.

She stared straight ahead at the white hole, wreathed with stars, into which they were about to plunge. Despite having friends on either side, she wrestled with her feelings alone.

It wasn't hope she felt. There was no way to change the past. The *Far Horizon* had vanished and the *New Dawn* and *Rising Star* were destroyed. Her parents were responsible for the mission and so they took the blame when it failed. That was the story people remembered; that the man responsible for the technology, and the woman commanding the fleet, her father and mother, were the two people most at fault when it failed.

But that's what I can change. I can't change the past but something else happened that day. It might still be happening. Someone had buried a secret about the mission, and it cost people their lives. I have the proof of that, and I'm going to find out the rest. I want to know. I need to know.

Then it was the *Rhino's* turn to enter the portal, and their ship flashed out of existence.

Tila realised at last it wasn't anticipation which gnawed at her stomach.

It wasn't nerves or fear that tightly gripped her will and compelled her forward.

Peter A Dixon

It wasn't hope she felt.
It was anger.
Someone has lied to me, she decided, *and I'm going to discover the truth.*

Thank you

Thanks for reading *The Juggernaut*!

I hope you enjoyed it.

As an independent author, reviews are really important to me, so I'd greatly appreciate it if you can take a moment to leave one on the site where you bought this book.

It doesn't have to be long, just say you can't wait to find out what happens next!

And if you really can't wait, just turn the page.

Your special offer

The second book in the series, *Parador*, will be released soon.

But if you can't want to find out where Tila's discovery leads, you can register for a FREE preview copy here,

www.peteradixon.com/sign-up

I'll also let you know when the final version is ready for publication.

Now, read on for an exclusive preview of *Parador*....

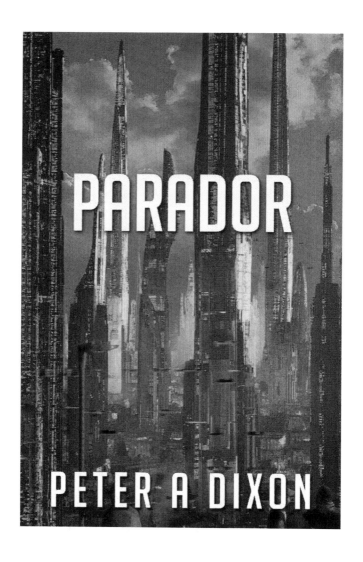

Parador

When Tila Vasquez discovered an impossible ship buried deep within the ruined space city of the Juggernaut, she uncovered hidden data which revealed that there was more to the story of the accident which had claimed the lives of her parents twelve years ago.

Now these secrets have taken her to Parador, the wealthiest planet among the Commonwealth systems. Here, decisions are made on trade and business which affect the lives of billions.

Along with her friends Malachi and Ellie, Tila will find that both new friends and new enemies stand in their way.

And there are some who will do anything to keep their secrets hidden.

www.peteradixon.com/books/parador

Exclusive extract from Parador

Jayce downed what was left in his glass (not for courage, he told himself) and leaned over to Ellie. "Wanna get out of here?"

Ellie grinned into her cup. A quick glance around told her that Tila was nowhere in sight. She nodded and set her cup down. "Where are we going?"

"Let's go for a ride. We can get out of the party for a while. No one will notice. We can take my racer."

Ellie nodded again, her insides churning. "Ok," she said. She didn't know if she was nervous about leaving alone with Jayce or excited for another ride in his racer. They slipped off their chairs and walked toward the garage. Ellie felt Jayce's fingers shyly brush against the back of her hand but she kept her eyes forward and her hands to herself.

There was still no sign of Malachi, which was beginning to worry her, and she couldn't see Tila anywhere either, although that was more of a relief than a concern. Tila had been even more prickly than usual tonight and she had made it very clear she was not interested in making new friends here on Parador.

But that doesn't mean I shouldn't.

They passed through the garden on their way to the garage. By now the guests had dispersed throughout the impressive grounds surrounding the opulent house and Ellie began to appreciate just how much land there was within the perimeter wall.

Trees and plants surrounded them in a way which suggested careful planning, not wild growth. The path they followed curved through the garden around flowerbeds, under green canopies and even over a small bridge which spanned a stream. The water bubbled and splashed happily over the rocks below them.

"You really own all of this?" she said in awe.

"Technically, no. Everything here is an asset of the corporation, but we get to live here and we can do what we want with the land, within reason of course.

Ellie made a dismissive gesture at the technicality, "But you get to live here."

Jayce nodded and looked at her, "It's good to be surrounded by beautiful things."

Ellie nodded too, still looking around at the garden, then realised that Jayce was still looking at her, and what he really meant. She blushed, grateful for the deepening shadows to hide her smile.

"Is that the garage?" she asked quickly and grateful for the distraction. She started toward a low building near the brick wall.

As soon as her back was turned Jayce kicked a stone off the path in frustration.

"Yeah." He hoped his voice didn't betray his disappointment at the lost moment as he followed her.

Ellie walked quickly to the door she had spotted, forcing Jayce to hurry to keep up with her. She looked back at the way they had come, worked something out in her head, and frowned. "I thought we arrived on the other side of the house."

"We did. That was the guest garage. This is where we keep our private vehicles. Wanna see?"

He touched the door control with one hand while the other optimistically reached out again for Ellie's.

The doors parted to reveal Tila. She stood with her own hand raised, as if she was just about to open the door from the other side.

She looked at them blankly, surprised for just a second to see them standing there. Together.

She looked at Ellie, then she looked at Jayce, then at their hands, then back at Jayce, and frowned.

Tila grabbed Ellie's hand before Jayce could reach it and pulled her into the garage. Jayce followed.

"Hey!" protested Ellie.

Tila ignored her complaint. "We've got a problem."

Ellie snatched back her hand. Tila's paranoia was getting out of control. "What is it now?" she said.

Tila turned back to the door, looked around quickly to see if anyone else was coming, then closed it, locked it, and leaned against it for support. She closed her eyes and muttered something Ellie couldn't hear. She assumed it was another complaint about Jayce.

"Well?" said Ellie. "What's the problem this time."

Tila opened her eyes.

"Malachi's missing."

About the Author

Peter has always been a fan of action and adventure stories, and science fiction and fantasy books, movies and TV shows. His first book, *The Juggernaut*, grew from a seed planted fifteen years ago, about a city in space built from the wrecks of hundreds of spaceships.

Since attending university in London, Peter has developed a background in media production, finance, and marketing for firms in the UK and internationally.

He believes heroes should always beat villains, thinks music provides the greatest inspiration, and writes to tell the stories he wants to live.

Peter is based in London, but divides his time between New England and the UK (old England - although over here we just call it England).

Printed in Great Britain
by Amazon